IGUANA BOY

I'D LIKE TO DEDICATE THIS BOOK TO MY MUM AND DAD.
THEY MADE ME AND I MADE THIS BOOK, SO IN SOME
WAYS THEY WROTE IT TOO. BASICALLY, THAT MEANS
MY MUM AND DAD PRETTY MUCH WRITE FART JOKES,
AND THEY CALL ME IMMATURE!

J.B.

FOR MIKE LITHERLAND, THE BEST ILLUSTRATION TUTOR, EVER.
THANK YOU KINDLY FOR INTRODUCING ME TO ALL THINGS
DIP-PEN AND INDIAN INK RELATED.

R.P.

IGUANA BOY

AND THE
GOLDEN
TOOTHBRUSH

JAMES BISHOP

AND ILLUSTRATED BY RIKIN PAREKH

Hodder
Children's
Books

HODDER CHILDREN'S BOOKS
FIRST PUBLISHED IN GREAT BRITAIN IN 2019 BY HODDER AND STOUGHTON
1 3 5 7 9 10 8 6 4 2
TEXT COPYRIGHT © JAMES BISHOP 2019
ILLUSTRATIONS © RIKIN PAREKH 2019
THE MORAL RIGHTS OF THE AUTHOR AND ILLUSTRATOR HAVE BEEN ASSERTED.

A CIP CATALOGUE RECORD FOR THIS BOOK
IS AVAILABLE FROM THE BRITISH LIBRARY.

ISBN 978 1 444 95096 0

PRINTED AND BOUND IN GREAT BRITAIN BY
CLAYS LTD, ELCOGRAF S.P.A.

THE PAPER AND BOARD USED IN THIS BOOK
ARE MADE FROM WOOD FROM RESPONSIBLE SOURCES.

MIX
Paper from
responsible sources
FSC
www.fsc.org   FSC® C104740

HODDER CHILDREN'S BOOKS
AN IMPRINT OF
HACHETTE CHILDREN'S GROUP
PART OF HODDER AND STOUGHTON
CARMELITE HOUSE
50 VICTORIA EMBANKMENT
LONDON EC4Y 0DZ

AN HACHETTE UK COMPANY
WWW.HACHETTE.CO.UK

WWW.HACHETTECHILDRENS.CO.UK

CONTENTS

Arctic
Thunder

Millie
Monday

Terrifying
Suzanne

Atomic Adam

Ron
Strongman

MEET THE CITD

SUPERHERO COLLECTIVE HQ ID PASS

NAME: DYLAN SPENCER

AKA: IGUANA BOY

SUPERPOWER: TALKING TO IGUANAS

AGE/HEIGHT: 9yrs/4ft 3ins

DISGUISE: CAPE!

FAVOURITE ANIMAL:
IGUANAS

FAVOURITE PIZZA TOPPING:
TRIPLE CHEESE

SUPERHERO COLLECTIVE HQ ID PASS

NAME: CHRIS

AKA: VENTRILOCHRIS

SUPERPOWER:
VOICE THROWING

AGE/HEIGHT: 10yrs/3ft 2ins

DISGUISE: SNAZZY JUMPSUIT

FAVOURITE HOBBY: WHISPERING
TO PEOPLE 20 METRES AWAY

SUPERHERO COLLECTIVE HQ ID PASS

NAME: **IFFI & FIFI**

AKA: **TELEPATHY TWINS**

SUPERPOWER:
TELEPATHY (WITH EACH OTHER)

AGE/HEIGHT: **12yrs/5ft**

DISGUISE: **N/A**

FAVOURITE PASTIME:
THINKING OUT LOUD

SUPERHERO COLLECTIVE HQ ID PASS

NAME: **SUZANNE**

AKA: **TERRIFYING SUZANNE**

SUPERPOWER:
BEING TERRIFYING

AGE/HEIGHT: **7yrs/3ft 5ins**

DISGUISE: **N/A**

FAVOURITE HOBBY: **SHOUTING**

CHAPTER 1

MAKING A SUPERHERO

Throughout the ages, since the dawn of time, a debate has raged amongst the human race:

'What is the best EVER superpower?!?'

It's something that has been passionately discussed ever since the very first superheroes emerged, a very (VERY) long time ago ...

No one has ever been able to agree what the best power is, however, over time, it

2

has been very clear what makes a rubbish
superpower ...

Yes, throughout history, the debate has raged on over the best superpower, but everyone pretty much agrees that if your power is the ability to talk to one useless animal, well, it doesn't get much worse ...

Dylan Spencer was at school, slumped in his chair, his head resting on the desk. School was not where he wanted to be. Perhaps this is a feeling MOST kids can relate to, but it was even worse for a superhero. All Dylan wanted to do was be out of the classroom, saving the world.

Having recently captured a supervillain named Repeat Offender (who actually turned out to be a good guy), Dylan was in the good books of his boss, Ron Strongman, the Head of the Superhero Collective. Dylan's department, the CITD (which stands for Cats In Trees Department), were no longer only being sent out to save cats from trees (the WORST job for a superhero). Instead, they were also being asked to take on actual real-life supervillains.

Only, things hadn't been going so well. Every time Iguana Boy and the CITD went out on a mission they would fail. EPICALLY. In fact, they hadn't captured one single supervillain since Repeat Offender; they were on a pretty awful losing streak, one that had put Dylan and his iguanas firmly in Ron Strongman's bad books and, along with the rest of the CITD, they had found themselves back on Cats In Trees duty.

Dylan had once again become the laughing stock of Superhero HQ, but it wasn't just his fellow superheroes who found Iguana Boy amusing. He also had to endure the giggles of his entire class, whenever the subject of superheroes came up at school.

'Every day someone, somewhere, is saved by a superhero,' said Mrs McGettigan, peering at the class over her bright red spectacles. 'When you really think about it, isn't that truly *extraordinary*?'

'It's not extraordinary,' said Charlie, a rather burly kid in Dylan's class.

'Here we go again …' muttered Dylan, who had seen Charlie Logan challenge Mrs McGettigan countless times before. He once argued that the sun and moon were the same thing because you never see them in the same place at the same time.

Mrs McGettigan sighed heavily, rose from her seat and perched on the edge of her desk ready to go to battle with Charlie Logan once more.

'Everyone knows there are hundreds of superheroes, and their job is to SAVE PEOPLE, so of course they are going to do it every day,' said Charlie.

'But don't you think, Charlie Logan, that the fact we HAVE people with such wonderful and inventive powers is truly extraordinary?' said Mrs McGettigan.

'Sure, I guess some powers are pretty cool ...' said Charlie, steering the conversation rather nicely. It was every kid's favourite topic, and Mrs McGettigan had walked straight into it once again.

'Super-strength!' shouted one kid, a pencil in either hand being lifted to his shoulders as if they weighed a ton.

'Super-speed!' said another, grabbing a piece of paper from the girl sitting next to him and waving it above his head. It said, 'Kim loves René' and had a picture of her and René holding hands encircled by a love heart. Kim looked incredibly embarrassed and the class laughed hysterically.

'Flying is by far the best!' said a girl with jet black hair, getting on top of her desk and jumping as high as she could, landing with a thud on the floor.

'Talking to iguanas!' shouted Charlie. And there it was, the inevitable Iguana Boy joke. Half the class fell off their chairs laughing. Even Mrs McGettigan let out a little chuckle.

'Arghh! Charlie makes that joke every single day. It wasn't funny the first time,' said Dylan frustratedly.

'You don't like my jokes?' taunted Charlie menacingly.

'It was a rubbish joke,' said Pauline, who was communicating with Dylan over radio. Dylan had an earpiece so that Superhero HQ could contact him in case of an emergency, and the iguanas had stolen one of the headsets from Ron Strongman's office so they could talk to Dylan when he was at school. It was incredibly annoying.

'Yeah, don't just sit there, Dylan, tell him Iguana Boy is awesome!' added Crazy Red-Eye Paul.

'Tell him about that time we brought down Repeat Offender,' added Paul, wrestling with the other iguanas for control of the microphone.

'Yeah, maybe you should tell him that

Iguana Boy captured Repeat Offender, who happened not to be a villain and now he's one of the best-loved superheroes at HQ. Everyone loves the Outtatime Kid,' said Pauline. Dylan could just about hear her in the background, above the rustling that Dylan could only imagine was the sound of the iguanas wrestling for control of the microphone.

'Well?' said Charlie, who was yet to get a reply as Dylan was momentarily distracted by his iguana pals. 'Why are you just standing there not saying anything, rather than laughing at my jokes like everyone else, LOSER?'

'I ... just think that ...' Dylan took another look at Charlie Logan, who was now out of his seat. He was a big kid. A REALLY big, intimidating kid. Dylan swallowed hard. 'I guess it was pretty funny ...' said Dylan, feeling defeated.

'So you think Iguana Boy is pretty stupid too?'

'Don't say it, kid,' said Smelly Paul.

'Oh no, he's going to say it!' said Paul,

before adding, 'Smelly Paul, you smell really bad today, like an ostrich fart.'

Dylan momentarily laughed to himself, thinking of Smelly Paul and remembering the fact that ostrich farts are the WORST-smelling farts in the animal kingdom. It's why they bury their heads underground all the time, to escape their own rotten stench. This laugh looked like he was agreeing with Charlie, that Iguana Boy really was stupid.

There was nothing else for it. 'Yes, he's pretty stupid.' Dylan hung his head.

'Well, I don't think he's stupid,' said Cara, the girl who was sitting next to Dylan. 'He's a superhero who has saved the world on more than one occasion. I personally think he deserves some respect.'

The class laughed, but it didn't seem to bother Cara. She looked over at Dylan and smiled. He couldn't remember the last time someone at school had smiled at him. It felt nice.

'I like her,' said Pauline over the earpiece.

'Now, if you are done educating the class about superpowers, Charlie ...' said Mrs McGettigan, but unfortunately Charlie wasn't finished.

'You're all wrong,' said Charlie. 'The best superpower,' he added with confidence, 'is not super-strength.'

The boy with the pencils dropped them miserably to the floor.

'It's not super-speed either,' Charlie went on. The boy who had grabbed the drawing from Kim screwed it up and threw it back at her.

'And it's definitely not being able to fly.' The girl who had jumped off her desk sat back down grumpily, resting her head in her hands.

'So, it's invisibility then, very good, now let's get on with the class, shall we?' said Mrs McGettigan.

'*Invisibility*? Don't be ridiculous!' said Charlie, moving to the front of the class. He gestured for Mrs McGettigan to move out the way and she duly obliged.

'I hate it when he does this,' whispered

Cara to Dylan. At first Dylan ignored it, assuming she was talking under her breath to herself, but when he looked over, she was looking directly at him.

'Uh … yeah … he's a complete wibbleflop,' said Dylan without thinking.

'Wibbleflop?' said Paul. 'Who uses the word *"wibbleflop"*?!? What even is that? Way to lose a friend before you've even made one there, mate.'

'I mean tool, idiot, stupid … face …'

Cara giggled. 'I prefer wibbleflop. It's a good word. Describes him perfectly.' She leaned in a little closer. 'Don't let him bully you, you're a much better person than him. Don't be afraid to stand up for what you

believe in. You're right, his jokes ARE NOT funny.' Dylan smiled.

'Then what is it already?!?' said Mrs McGettigan impatiently. Despite her annoyance, she seemed genuinely interested in the answer and had now sat down in Charlie's empty seat at the front of the class.

'It's the power of persuasion.' The class looked confused.

'The power of persuasion? You mean like that supervillain has ... what's his name again ...' said a rather thoughtful-looking boy at the front of the class.

'Mind Bender,' said Charlie confidently. 'Exactly. It's the BEST power. Just imagine the thing you want most in the world ...'

'To be rich!'

'A pony!'

'For the school bell to ring,' said Dylan under his breath. Cara chuckled and high-fived him.

'To regain control of my class,' said Mrs McGettigan, scratching her head.

'A ham and pickle sandwich!' The class turned to look at the boy who had shouted. 'What? I'm hungry …' he said weakly.

'Good, good. Those are all excellent answers,' Mrs McGettigan said. 'Well, apart from the ham and pickle sandwich – seriously, dream bigger, Doug. Now can we all do some work?'

Charlie ignored her and continued. 'Think

of it this way, you are only one conversation away from getting those things. All you need to do is use the right words, at the right time, to convince the person who already owns that thing, and they could give you whatever you want. Thousands of pounds. Even a pony.'

'Or a sandwich,' said Doug.

'Fine, or a sandwich ... And if you had the power of persuasion ...'

'They would have to give it to you!' Mrs McGettigan began to clap. The rest of the class followed. Except Dylan, who wasn't exactly happy with his classmates for celebrating the powers of a supervillain. Ron Strongman would be outraged if he knew

Dylan wasn't trying to convince his class to turn against a supervillain.

'Mind Bender is a supervillain, and his powers are NOT cool,' he said stubbornly.

Charlie Logan left his spot at the front of the class and approached Dylan's desk. He cut an imposing figure, having clearly had a growth spurt before all the other kids. He towered over Dylan, placing his huge fists on his desk, before lowering his head so that their eyes were just a few centimetres apart.

'I strongly suggest you reconsider what you just said and agree with me,' said Charlie, getting out some jelly babies and eating them while keeping his eyes firmly on Dylan.

'On second thoughts, I agree: persuasion

is the best power, and it doesn't matter that the power belongs to a supervillain who has been causing chaos across London for months.'

'See! I persuaded him to agree with me!' Charlie spun on his heels and smiled to the rest of the class. 'Maybe I have the power!' he said.

'I'm pretty sure that was a threat,' said Pauline.

'Yeah, that doesn't count as a superpower,' added Paul.

'I don't know, sounded pretty persuasive to me,' said Crazy Red-Eye Paul.

'You don't have any powers, Charlie Logan, you're just a bully,' said Cara defiantly, standing up for Dylan. Charlie didn't refute her claim. He simply smiled and walked back to the front of the class.

Dylan hung his head in shame, disappointed to have given in so easily. A good superhero would have stood behind their words and faced the consequences, he thought, but he had buckled at the mere sight of Charlie Logan menacingly munching on a packet of jelly babies.

Cara sat down and looked at Dylan, but he wouldn't meet her eye. He was too embarrassed. She leaned over. 'I don't like bullies and he had no right to speak to you like that. You're ...' She trailed off. 'At least in MY opinion ... you're a pretty super guy,

Dylan. You just need to believe in yourself.'

Dylan forced a smile, but felt utterly embarrassed. He wasn't entirely sure why the girl one desk over was suddenly being so nice to him, but he appreciated it.

Charlie returned to his seat and touched Mrs McGettigan on the shoulder. 'You can take it from here.' Their teacher looked a little flustered, as if she wasn't prepared to retake the reins so soon, and muttered to herself as she made her way to the front of the class.

As Cara reached out to put a reassuring hand on Dylan's shoulder, he raised a hand to his ear, pushing Cara away. It was Ron Strongman calling over his earpiece, his loud voice booming into his ear.

'Calling all members of the CITD, do you read me?'

No reply. 'Ah, yes of course, you're all at … what's it called again … the place where you learn stuff … SCHOOL! That's the one. Forgot you can't reply. If you can hear me, cough.'

Dylan coughed gently.

'Oh dear, Iguana Boy, are you sick?' said Ron, sounding frustrated. 'That simply won't do, you have an important mission to attend to!'

'No, sir, you asked me to cough if I could hear you,' whispered Dylan, turning his back to Cara so she wouldn't overhear.

'Did I? Ah yes, of course! That does sound like something I would say, very good. Now then, we have an emergency in Hyde Park by the lake.'

'I'm honoured you thought of me, sir,' said Dylan, happy to FINALLY be back in Ron Strongman's good books.

'Told you it was a matter of time, kid,' said Paul reassuringly.

'Back in the game, buddy!' added Red-Eye.

'Yes, yes, of course, no one better. Get that team of yours over there right away. The poor cat has been stuck in the tree all night and is terribly hungry.'

'Oh …' said Dylan. It wasn't a super-important mission after all. It was just another stupid cat stuck in an extra-stupid tree.

'Go indeed! Good luck, Iguana Kid. Oh and make sure you get that cough sorted before you come back to Superhero HQ. I don't want you passing your lurgy around the office. Good luck, team,' said Ron and he was gone.

Dylan's hand went to his stomach immediately, the other flying into the air simultaneously.

'Yes, Dylan?' said Mrs McGettigan.

'I have a stomach ache, may I see the school nurse please?' said Dylan.

Mrs McGettigan waved her hand towards

the door dismissively and carried on talking to the class.

'Are you OK?' asked Cara.

'Uh … yeah, just a bit of a stomach bug,' said Dylan.

'OK, well be careful,' Cara said.

'Careful, why would I need to be careful?'

'You know … if it's a stomach bug … maybe head to the toilet first?' Dylan went a deep shade of red, thanked her for the advice and left the class as quickly as possible, heading straight out the door and towards Hyde Park.

CHAPTER 2

THE ICE CREAM THIEF

When Dylan arrived at the park, after swinging by his house to pick up the iguanas, he was surprised by what he saw. In the middle of the park was a HUGE ball of ice cream that stood at least twelve metres high. It was pretty close to the top of one of the trees. He arrived just in time to see a cat casually jump off a branch on to the ice cream, before effortlessly sliding down to the ground.

'Well, that solves *that* problem,' said Dylan to the iguanas.

Dylan had been so in awe of the sheer size of the ice cream ball that he hadn't noticed what was going on at the base. There was

a flurry of action, literally people throwing themselves at the ice cream face first, and as he approached, he noticed his team: the CITD.

There standing closest to the ice cream were the Telepathy Twins, Iffi and Fifi. They could be quite infuriating as they had the rather annoying superpower of reading each other's minds. It often resulted in them having a conversation with each other in their own heads, completely oblivious to the fact they weren't talking out loud. The Telepathy Twins were scooping out handfuls of the gloopy ice cream and throwing it at each other. Hardly productive, thought Dylan.

Next to them was Terrifying Suzanne. Dylan was always a little wary of her, because, well, she was simply terrifying. No one really knew if she had a power or if she was just really, really scary by accident. In some ways it didn't much matter. She was screaming at the ice cream, as if she expected it to melt in terror.

Finally, there was VentriloChris. He could throw his voice in a million different directions, which at times could prove pretty useful. Unfortunately, he wasn't the brightest knife in the drawer (a phrase he would often use, thus proving his own point ...) and would often fail to use his powers appropriately. In fact, mostly he just talked.

A lot. Though he would have a hard time talking right now, thought Dylan, as he had stepped forward to all but bury his face in the ball of ice cream.

'That looks pretty incredible,' said Paul, licking his nose with his tongue. 'That section looks like mint choc chip to me!'

'Wait, guys, it must be the work of the Ice Cream Thief!' said Dylan, suddenly putting it all together. He had heard all about this supervillain; everyone had.

'The supervillain that stops ice cream from melting?' said Paul.

'Oh yeah! He gathers it into large balls like this, which he then rolls down hills causing mass destruction in towns and

34

cities,' added Pauline.

'Wow, that's really dumb. If I could stop ice cream from melting, I'd just eat it all day long!' said Red-Eye.

'He must be close by!' said Dylan, scanning the area. 'And we can't stand idly by …' Dylan sprang into action, before realising that he was the only one doing anything. The rest of the CITD hadn't even noticed he was there. They were gorging themselves on ice cream instead. Dylan looked at them all, and considered telling them off, but then remembered how much of a tough time they had been having, trying and failing at their missions.

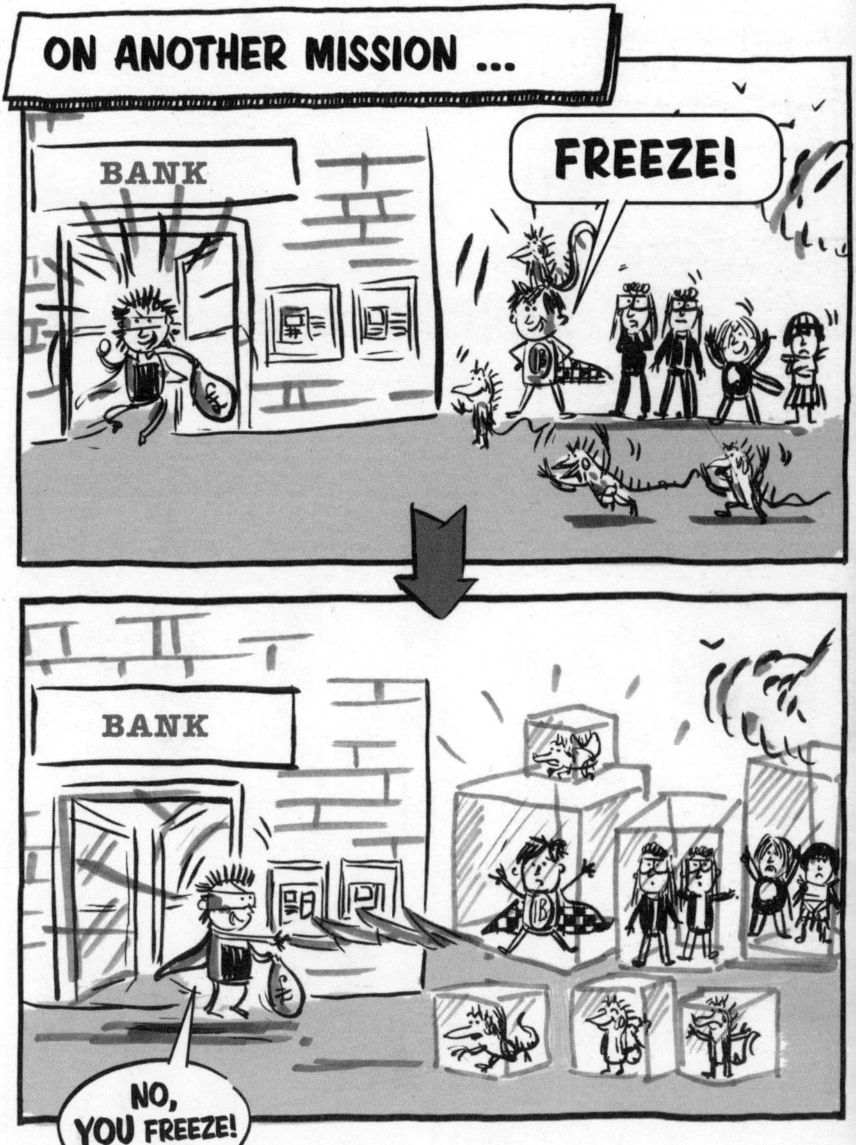
ON ANOTHER MISSION ...
BANK
FREEZE!
BANK
NO, YOU FREEZE!

It had been tough, but perhaps this was their shot at redemption. Dylan clapped his hands, but it didn't seem to get the attention of any of the CITD.

'Has anyone seen the Ice Cream Thief?' said Dylan loudly. Still nothing.

'Has anyone even looked?' added Paul.

'It looks like VentriloChris is trying to find him inside the ball of ice cream,' said Red-Eye. 'Perhaps I should help him.'

'Excellent idea,' said Paul, and they flung themselves at the giant ball of ice cream with a flick of their tails, landing smack bang in the middle. They buried their heads inside and let themselves slide gently down.

'Guys, seriously, has anyone seen the

supervillain?!' repeated Dylan desperately.

'Yeah, he's that kid over by the swings,' said Iffi.

'The one with the massive monobrow and Elton John style sunglasses,' added Fifi.

Dylan threw his arms into the air in a 'why do I even bother?' motion. Of course, the Telepathy Twins had found the supervillain, but had failed to say so out loud (as per usual) which wasn't particularly helpful.

It didn't matter, because moments later the supervillain skipped past Dylan and his merry band of superheroes holding a huge cone of ice cream, which was at least three times taller than Dylan. He was whistling to himself, and as he brushed past Dylan, he tipped his sunglasses and gave him a little 'how do you do' nod.

The supervillain threw the ice cream on to the growing mound and as soon as it had landed, VentriloChris began massaging it into the ball. The supervillain skipped back past Dylan, tipped his sunglasses once more and smiled.

'What are you doing?' said Dylan, pulling VentriloChris away.

'Oh hey, Iguana Boy!' said VentriloChris, completely surprised to see him. 'I'm just making sure it all sticks together properly.'

'But it's being put together by a supervillain!'

'Yeah, but you don't want it all to fall

apart, it's practically a work of art!'

'I LOVE ICE CREAM!'

screamed Terrifying Suzanne.

'See! Even Terrifying Suzanne is on board.'

'I don't know why I even bother talking to any of you sometimes,' said Dylan, turning away. Once more it looked like he was going to have to try and capture the supervillain without the CITD. Not entirely on his own of course …

'Come on, Dylan, get after him,' said Pauline.

'He went that way,' said Smelly Paul, pointing to Dylan's left. He was sitting on Dylan's shoulder, so when he pointed, Smelly Paul's armpit was thrust into Dylan's face.

'Have you been playing with a large group of ostriches recently?'

'No. What an odd question!' said Smelly Paul.

'We don't have time to mess about, we can't afford to mess up again!' said Pauline who was sitting on Dylan's other shoulder, fidgeting nervously.

'You're right, we could really use a win. Let's go and get him,' said Dylan.

Dylan, Pauline and Smelly Paul headed over to the Ice Cream Thief, who was just approaching a little boy holding a rather juicy-looking ice cream cone. He looked particularly pleased with himself as he had managed to slide down the slide without dropping his ice cream.

The Ice Cream Thief approached, snatched the ice cream and held it in the air triumphantly. The boy's bottom lip began to quiver, and then he let out a humungous wail.

'Not so fast,' said Dylan, holding his hand out in front of him in a stopping motion.

'OK ...' said the Ice Cream Thief, who then began to walk incredibly slowly towards Dylan.

'What are you doing?' asked Dylan.

'Yoooooouuuuuuuuuuuu.................... saaaaaaiiiiiiiiiiiiddddddddd.................... nnnnnnnooooooooottttttt..................

'I meant stop what you are doing, not

slow down.'

'Oh, I see. In that case, no.' Dylan hadn't been expecting that.

'Give him what for, Dylan!' said Pauline, snarling her teeth.

'Yeah, show him you don't mess with Iguana Boy,' said Smelly Paul, lifting both of his arms in the air and pointing them towards the Ice Cream Thief. It forced him to take a couple of steps backwards.

'I really hope it doesn't turn out this kid can breathe fire ...' said Paul hesitantly.

'You can't say no to me,' said Dylan.

'No, I can say no and there is NOthing you can do about it. Also no,' said the Ice Cream Thief.

'Right, you leave me no choice ...' Dylan walked over to the Ice Cream Thief, who was a similar age to Dylan and, on approach, he realised quite a bit bigger. In fact, he reminded him of Charlie Logan quite a lot.

Dylan went to grab his arm, but the Ice Cream Thief nonchalantly slapped his hand away, giving the ice cream a small lick at the same time. Dylan then tried to grab him with both arms, but the supervillain pushed him in the chest with his free hand, sending him flying to the ground. Another lick.

'This isn't going well,' said Pauline.

'Bet you wish you had super-strength, don't you, kid?' added Paul.

'Yeah, or the power of persuasion!'

added Red-Eye.

The Ice Cream Thief loomed over him, casting an imposing shadow over his entire body. Dylan suddenly felt utterly helpless. It was the same feeling he had felt earlier that day when Charlie Logan had intimidated him into agreeing that Iguana Boy was stupid, and that the power of persuasion was the best superpower.

He was about to lie down and admit defeat when he heard a light whisper in his ear.

'You can do it, Iguana Boy. Believe in yourself ...'

The mysterious voice was right. Enough was enough. Perhaps it was his subconscious telling him to stand up for himself, but whatever it was, it was enough to get Dylan back up on his feet.

As he picked himself up off the ground, he felt rage surging through his body. It began in his feet and worked its way up his legs. He felt it bubbling in his stomach as it rose to his chest, his heart thumping at super-speed. It travelled down his arms, his palms clenching into rock-solid fists, before finally it made its way to his temples, where it pulsated furiously. His teeth ground, his brain fuzzled, his nose snorted and his eyes glazed over in a fine red mist ...

Dylan let out a short, sharp grunt, followed by a blood-curdling scream, and ran as fast as he could, head bowed, towards his enemy.

The Ice Cream Thief held out his hand as he braced for impact, and Dylan went crashing into him head first.

CHAPTER 3

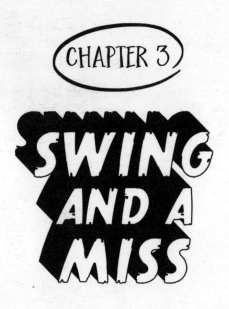

SWING AND A MISS

The next day, Iguana Boy was all over the front page of the *London Bugle*. He couldn't believe it. The CITD had been in a bit of a funk as of late and now here he was, in Ron Strongman's office, looking at a picture of himself on the front page of the biggest newspaper in London …

LONDON 🎺 BUGLE

Photo: R. Parekh

ANOTHER SWING AND A MISS FOR IGUANA BOY AND THE CITD

UNBELIEVABLE though it may seem, Iguana Boy has once again been defeated by a supervillain. Iguana Boy made an embarrassing attempt to defeat the Ice Cream Thief yesterday to no avail. Luckily, Millie Monday and Arctic Thunder swooped in to save the day, wiping the smile off the Ice Cream Thief's face. But how long can Iguana Boy stay a superhero after failing so many missions? We asked Ron Strongman, leader of the Superhero Collective to comment. "I will always stand by my superheroes. It seems Iguana Boy was just having an off day. If his bad luck continues, however, I will have no choice but to send him to a special superhero workshop at Sundae school."

It had been a disaster. It turned out that even in full-rage mode, running at full speed, putting every ounce of strength he had into it, Dylan was still incredibly weak. His head had hit the hand of the Ice Cream Thief, who had caught his forehead like it was a ball. Dylan kept trying to drive forward, but it was no use, he had lost all momentum. He swung his arms up but it was a lesson in futility as he couldn't reach the supervillain, who was keeping him at arm's distance with ease.

Little did Dylan know, a photographer who had been taking photos of the local wildlife had captured the whole thing. What was worse, he had also captured Millie

Monday and Arctic Thunder turning up to save the day, and all the things the CITD were getting up to at the time of the crime.

'What am I going to do with you, Iguana Kid?' Dylan didn't dare correct him. Ron read out the headline: '*Another swing and a miss for Iguana Boy and the CITD.*' Ron sighed heavily. 'I sent you over there to get a cat down from a tree and then ...' Ron tapped the front page of the paper.

'Well, I couldn't stand idly by ...' said Dylan, testing the waters. Ron stared blankly at him.

'And technically the cat did get down from the tree,' said Paul.

'I'm so sorry, sir, it won't happen again.' Dylan bowed his head, as did all of the iguanas, who were perching on his shoulders. They had insisted on being there for moral support.

'Oh good, good, it won't happen again. Perfect. Excellent,' said Ron with a bucketful of sarcasm. Paul and Pauline high-fived, Smelly Paul clapped his hands and Red-Eye … well, no one is quite sure exactly what he did, but the closest description would probably be dancing energetically, before gnawing on his own leg.

Here's the thing about sarcasm. Iguanas really don't get it. It's one of those human things they simply don't understand. Dylan stared at the ground and hoped that Ron Strongman hadn't noticed their inappropriate celebrations.

'Your little chameleon creatures think this is amusing, do they?' boomed Ron. He had noticed.

'Uh, no, sir …'

'Exactly what aren't you going to do again?' continued Ron. 'Because you said "it won't happen again" the last time you were in my office, and the time before that, and if I am not mistaken, the time before that. So, it can't be failing to catch a supervillain. Are you perhaps suggesting that you won't let a supervillain hold your head and make you look like a fool?'

'Well yes, *that* certainly won't happen again …'

'Oh good, excellent.' This time the iguanas only half celebrated as they were feeling a little uncertain. Well, Red-Eye hadn't really stopped to be honest, he was still going to

town on his leg.

'Do you know how much trouble you have caused me? Thank goodness your brother and sister were there to bail you out. AGAIN.' Ron sighed heavily. 'This is your last chance. One more mistake, and you and your friends will have to leave the Superhero Collective for good.'

Ron perched on the edge of his desk and bent down so his head was level with Dylan's. He gently put his hand under his chin, and lifted Dylan's head up. 'Look, Iguana Kid, I like you. I'm still not a fan of your weird lizard friends …'

Dylan instinctively held on to Pauline's tail behind his back. It was a good move as she was ready to launch herself at him.

'Your heart is in the right place and you try harder than any superhero I have ever met.'

'Thank you, sir,' said Dylan, blushing.

'But maybe that isn't enough. Maybe you just don't have what it takes to be a superhero.' These words cut like an axe through a chocolate gateau, splitting Dylan clean in two. One half was happy to hear that his idol had noticed how hard he tried. The other was devastated that all his effort could have been in vain.

'Now, I have a very important briefing to give, so I suggest you head over to the conference room now. Wouldn't want to be late, would you?'

Ron Strongman stood up and walked over to his office door. He opened it and gestured towards the exit. 'One more chance, Iguana Kid. One more chance.'

CHAPTER 4

THE GOLDEN TOOTHBRUSH

'OK, OK, settle down now,' said Ron Strongman to the superheroes that had gathered in the briefing room. Dylan was sitting in the front row, desperate to show he was listening keenly and willing to help.

'A certain supervillain is continuing to cause us quite a bit of trouble ...'

'Say no more,' said Arctic Thunder, Dylan's annoying brother, as he flew up to the stage and stood next to Ron Strongman. 'I'll take care of this supervillain,' he proclaimed proudly.

'Excellent. So, I don't need to give you any more information then?' said Ron.

'Uh ... well, I mean ...' Arctic Thunder was suddenly feeling quite flustered. Dylan forgot about his failure in the park for a moment and enjoyed watching his brother flounder. 'Maybe his name, yes, that would be good.'

'I see.'

'And his location would also be pretty handy.'

'Would it? Yes, yes.'

'And his superpower and any previous crimes committed would be great.'

'Of course, of course. Seems like you need some sort of briefing, would you say?'

'Yes, that would be great!'

'Then sit down.' Ron pointed towards the empty chair Arctic Thunder had vacated and he floated back to it, landing in a slump. Dylan noticed his sister Millie Monday stifle a laugh.

Once upon a time Arctic Thunder had been Ron's favourite superhero, and he could get away with just about anything, but he was no longer Ron's right-hand man, and every time he tried to impress him, he ended up doing the exact opposite.

Ron's new favourite hero was the Outtatime Kid, something Dylan was proud of. He used to be a supervillain, but Dylan had captured him, and helped set him on a new path. The path towards becoming a truly incredible superhero. He rarely got to see him though, as the Outtatime Kid was always off saving the world.

'Right, where was I? Ah yes, this supervillain. I am of course talking about Mind Bender who, as you all know, has the power of persuasion.' Dylan slapped his forehead. *This again, really?* he thought to himself. 'He has been a thorn in our side for the past few months now. Who can forget the time he persuaded Ed Sheeran to give up music to become a synchronised swimmer?'

'Oh, he was utterly awful,' said Millie Monday. 'Not synchronised AT ALL.'

'Quite right. Or the time he convinced the BBC to do a series of *Strictly Come Dancing* with horses instead of celebrities?' Ron seemed distracted.

'Actually, that was quite a good series, to be honest,' said Millie Monday. 'I still can't believe that Golden Star didn't win; she was robbed, I tell you, robbed!'

'Yes, yes, I agree with you Millie, I really do, but now, his misdemeanours have become much more serious. Let's just say our government is now compromised. Take a look at this footage from inside Ten Downing Street this morning.'

Ron's assistants rolled down the video screen.

10 DOWNING STREET. 8:00AM PRIME MINISTER'S MEETING.

The Prime Minister took a huge bite out of her Nutella-filled croissant and then banged it on the table. Nutella flew out and hit the Deputy Prime Minister on the side of his face, leaving a sticky blotch on his tie. He didn't flinch. It didn't look like this was the first time this had happened.

'ORDER, ORDER!' screamed the Prime Minister, shoving the remainder of her indulgent pastry into her gob. She then made the rest of her cabinet wait for her to chew her monster mouthful and swallow, before she formally kicked off the meeting.

'So, first order of business. Can we please buy some more Nutella; somebody has been putting far too much in their croissants and I had to practically scrape the bottom of the jar to reach the last remaining gooey goodness.'

'Yes, Prime Minister,' said a rather serious-looking gentleman on her left.

'Second order of business … let me see …' She was rifling through pages and pages in a big thick binder on the table, getting huge splodges of chocolate spread all over them. 'Ah yes, here we go, of course. So what's going on?'

'What's going on, Prime Minister?' asked the Deputy Prime Minister.

'Yes, you know, what's going on, in the country? Generally speaking.' They all looked at her with a high level of confusion, but before any of them had a chance to report on 'what's going on', the television screen at the end of the long conference table burst into life.

'Hello, Prime Minister,' said Mind Bender, who sat on a luxurious-looking blue velvet sofa in a fancy living room. He was sitting cross-legged, his belly popping out of his tight white supervillain outfit. He wore a mask which had two antennae, connected by a lightning bolt.

'What is the meaning of this?' said the Prime Minister, getting up from her chair, banging both fists on the table, accidentally hitting another Nutella-filled croissant and ruining the Deputy Prime Minister's jacket.

She looked a little closer at the screen; something seemed familiar to her. Then it hit her. She was surprised she hadn't recognised it straight away. After all, *Good Morning Dear – with Lauren Kelly* was one of her favourite TV shows, and that was definitely the sofa in Lauren Kelly's living room. The Prime Minister had bought one for her own house, she'd liked it so much.

For a small second she thought she might have been 'Kelly's Surprise Contestant'. Each week, Lauren Kelly would appear on an unsuspecting person's TV, inviting them to appear on another of her shows, *Kelly's Wellies*, that afternoon (during this show contestants would have to throw wellington boots into a variety of different things – car boots, moving shopping trolleys, laundry bins, toilets – to earn cash prizes).

The Prime Minister had always wanted to go on the show (she was pretty good at throwing wellies) but it soon became obvious that was not the reason for the interruption. She was now face to face with Mind Bender.

'What is the meaning of this?!?' said the Prime Minister, clearly irritated by being so rudely interrupted.

'Hello, Prime Minister, my name is Mind Bender and, well, I'm a supervillain.'

'Oh yes, Mind Bender. The man who made sure I would never get to enjoy another album by Ed Sheeran. How dare you interrupt my meeting! I'm a very busy and important person, don't you know!' The Prime Minister let out the hint of a smile as she said this.

'Oh, I know you are, Prime Minister, do forgive the intrusion, but as a supervillain, it's sort of my job. Just thought I would drop into your meeting, see how you're doing, take over your government by mind control, you know, usual supervillainy stuff.'

The Prime Minister cackled.

'Mind control? You think your fancy little mind games will work ON ME?!' She laughed even harder this time.

'On you, Prime Minister? Of course not! They only work on weak and susceptible people. They certainly don't work on cats. After all, you are a pussy cat, aren't you?' said Mind Bender with a wry smile.

The Prime Minister jumped up on to the desk and hissed at the Deputy Prime Minister. She then licked her hand and began pawing at her eye and scratching her neck.

The Foreign Secretary stared at her, his mouth wide open in shock. He pulled out his phone, took a photo and put the phone back in his pocket.

Mind Bender stopped the Prime Minister thinking she was a cat and she sat back down on her seat.

'You have our attention, Mind Bender. What are your demands?' she said.

'Uh ... Excellent. HA HA! I have you exactly where I want you,' said Mind Bender, rubbing his hands gleefully.

'You have us exactly where you want us,' said the Prime Minister submissively. 'What are your demands?' she repeated.

'I would like ... I need ... No, I DEMAND ... A new toothbrush.'

HA HA HA HA HA HA HA HA HA! Everyone in the government briefing room laughed hysterically.

'Uh ... an electric toothbrush, that is.'

More laughter.

'Made of gold.'

Laughter.

'And it needs to be able to turn into a plane which can take me anywhere in the world in forty-five seconds.'

The laughter stopped.

'But, Mind Bender, that's impossible ...'

'YOU HAVE MY DEMANDS!'

he screamed.

'We have your demands,' said the Prime Minister obligingly. She turned to the man on her right. 'Get the country's top scientists working on a golden toothbrush with the ability to turn into a plane and travel anywhere in the world in forty-five seconds.'

'And it has to be electric,' added Mind Bender.

'Of course,' said the Prime Minister.

(BACK TO THE BRIEFING ROOM ...)

'As you can see from this footage, our government is now working on building some sort of electric toothbrush, supersonic plane ...'

'Made of gold,' added Arctic Thunder.

'What it's made of really isn't important; in fact, *what it is,* isn't important. I'm not sure it's really that important to Mind Bender himself. The point is if they are throwing all of their resources into a single project, then they are ignoring all of the real issues facing our great country. We must stop Mind Bender at once.'

Ron Strongman looked out across the

room, his eyes falling on each hero as he decided who to send on this very important mission.

'Atomic Adam, Millie Monday, Lacey Shoestring and ...'

Dylan and Arctic Thunder both sat upright, smiling at Ron and desperately trying to appear as if they were well-behaved kids being selected for show and tell.

'Arctic Thunder.' Dylan sank into his chair as his brother punched the air. 'Bring him to justice, as soon as you can.'

Listen carefully to what I'm about to tell you, as it is extremely important. It is the story of the BIGGEST and BEST and most SUPER-AWESOME and OTHER WORDS THAT MAKE HIM SOUND COOL supervillain the world has ever seen.

He is POPULAR and SMART and needs

no introduction …

Oh wait, actually he DOES need an introduction, or you won't know who I'm talking about …

OK, in that case he needs a GRAND introduction. Drum roll please …

Wait. Reader, are you giving him a drum roll? Put down this book immediately if you're not and give the BIGGEST and BEST and most SUPER-AWESOME and OTHER WORDS THAT MAKE HIM SOUND COOL supervillain the world has ever seen, the introduction he DESERVES …

Keep drumming.

Louder.

LOUDER!

If your parents can't hear you all the way downstairs, then you are

NOT
DRUMMING
LOUDLY ENOUGH!

OK, that's better.

Now please welcome ...

Just look at him. Isn't he **AMAZING?!?**

If a bunch of super-brainy scientists locked themselves in a laboratory for a thousand years with the purpose of creating the perfect supervillain, Mind Bender would be the end result.

What's his power, I hear you ask? It's pretty **FANTASTIC**. He has the **AWESOME** power of persuasion.

It means he can get people to say or do just about anything, just by talking to them. Well, most people at least. He once got a kid in his class to throw rolled-up paper at his teacher every time they spoke; another time he managed to convince someone at a sleepover to do a HUGE fart under the duvet and then stay under there ALL NIGHT (they had eaten egg and beans for dinner too). And this one time, he even got a real-life author to write about how AMAZING he is in his book!

YESTERDAY

Mind Bender was standing in front of the mirror. He pulled down his shirt to cover his belly, but the shirt popped back up again, revealing some belly button fluff. He picked it out, gave it a good sniff, and then flicked it on to the floor. He was ready.

He turned round and sat down on the blue velvet sofa. It was surprisingly hard. He had always thought the sofa looked comfortable on the telly, but then again, he had always thought he was looking into someone's living room, in an actual house, not a big warehouse with no walls and a ceiling that seemed to stretch into space.

It made sense – why would Lauren Kelly invite people into her home every morning to film a TV show? From where he was sitting he could see the TV sets for some of his favourite shows: *Jungly Surprise* – a game show where kids had to search for coconuts across the jungle. The more coconuts, the bigger the surprise at the end of the show; *Let's Talk about Stuff* – a talk show where presenter Simon Daly would talk about, well, stuff (he had a thick Irish accent and

Mind Bender had a hard time understanding what was being talked about, but he liked it all the same); and of course, everyone's favourite show, *Kelly's Wellies*.

All these sets were under one roof, just a stone's throw away from each other (or a wellington boot's throw away ...). As Mind Bender looked around, learning all about the magic of TV, Lauren Kelly approached holding a mug of tea.

'Here you go, dear, a nice warm brew for you,' she said, passing over the mug of tea. Mind Bender took it, not bothering to thank her, and Lauren stood patiently, a glazed look in her eyes, waiting for further instruction.

'Sit, Lauren Kelly. Sit,' said Mind Bender,

patting the empty seat next to him. Lauren sat down as Mind Bender was once again picking out fluff from his belly button and giving it a good sniff.

'Tell me, Lauren Kelly from *Kelly's Wellies* on the telly, do I have a smelly belly? Smell me and tell me.'

Lauren Kelly leaned over and sniffed his belly.

'It's not great, dear,' she said.

'So, you would say I smell pretty good?'

'You smell pretty good!' she confirmed, seemingly changing her mind.

'Excellent. Always best to start the day feeling fresh. And what a day we have ahead of ourselves!' Mind Bender said, jumping off the sofa and flipping over a whiteboard to reveal the words 'Evil Plan'. Underneath them were a series of bullet points. 'Today I am going to reveal my Evil Plan. Are you ready?'

'Yes, dear,' said Lauren automatically.

'You see, it's quite simple. Step One: take over the Lauren Kelly show. That was pretty easy; I can tick that off the list.' Mind Bender put a little tick next to it on the board.

'Step Two: call the Prime Minister.' Mind Bender took a step back and rubbed his chin. 'I don't suppose you have the Prime Minister's number? You are both famous, after all.'

'I interviewed her last year, so I actually

do. Although not all celebrities know each other, dear, that's a bit of a rude assumption …'

'Excellent,' said Mind Bender, licking his lips. 'You can call her for me when the time comes. Step Three: get her under my control. I'll make her pretend to be a cat or something, see if she is susceptible to my power!' He took another step back and marvelled at his wonderful plan. 'It's a thing of beauty, isn't it?'

'Once you have her under your power, what next, dear?'

'Uh …' Mind Bender hadn't thought of that. 'Good point. I hadn't thought of that. What are my demands …?'

'Putting you through now, dear, please hold.'

'Wait, what, now?'

Mind Bender plonked himself on the sofa, but before he could tell her to stop the call, he was connected with the Prime Minister.

Luckily, the Prime Minister was susceptible to his power immediately, and he had her eating out of the palm of his hand (or should that be lapping milk?).

When the Prime Minister asked him his demands, however, he panicked.

He couldn't think of anything, and then he saw it. His shopping list, which was on a flipchart next to the whiteboard which housed his Evil Plan. At the very top was a new toothbrush.

It was a ridiculous demand, the laughter made sense, but now Mind Bender had said it, 'a new toothbrush', he had to own it. He would just have to make it a more lavish toothbrush …

The fact is, he didn't really care about what he was asking for. The problem with the power of persuasion is you very quickly get used to having whatever you want, and when you can have whatever you want, you start to not want anything at all. This left Mind Bender feeling incredibly BORED. The only way he could get over it was by having a little fun …

When he first developed his powers, the

idea of becoming a superhero, of using his powers to help others, didn't even cross his mind. He just thought of things that would amuse him, and did those instead. This was the same before he even had his powers.

One day he was given ten pounds by his mum to give to a charity of his choice. This was her little way of trying to teach him the value of helping others. He was left with a simple choice: to give the money to a charity, or pocket the cash and spend it on something for himself.

He chose neither of those options. Instead, he gave the ten pounds to another boy in his class to hold a snail in his mouth for sixty seconds. To him, this was hilarious and it was this approach that he seemed to bring into his supervillain activities.

He could have used his powers to take over the world or steal fat lumps of cash from banks, but instead, he thought it would be HILARIOUS to watch horses do ballroom dancing with people on TV. He had a point, it was pretty funny.

The truth is he hadn't really given much thought about what he was going to get the Prime Minister to do. He didn't have some grand intention of taking over the world. She just happened to be in the news a lot, and he thought it would be funny if he messed around with her a little.

He also thought it was pretty funny to

take over the Prime Minister's favourite TV show and get the star to make him tea and teach him how to throw wellies. It was whilst Lauren Kelly was teaching him a technique that would maximise the distance of his throw, that the first superheroes arrived.

BACK TO THE PRESENT

Mind Bender had been expecting this. After all, his taking over the government wouldn't go unnoticed, and he knew that all the superheroes would recognise the set of *Good Morning Dear – with Lauren Kelly*.

'Freeze,' demanded Millie Monday, holding out her hand in a stopping motion. Mind Bender picked up a welly, extended his arm

backwards
and propelled it
forwards. It landed on the
ground about a metre away from any of the
superheroes.

Lauren Kelly was confused and thought she was presenting the show. 'You let go too early, dear! No grand prize for you and I'm afraid that's all we have time for this week on *Kelly's Wellies* ...' Mind Bender took a moment to think that perhaps constant mind control had an adverse effect on people, before returning his attention to the heroes in front of him.

'Was that aimed at us?' asked Atomic Adam, genuinely unsure.

'I hope not, truly awful throw,' added Arctic Thunder, striding forward and picking up the boot.

'Urgh, I hate those awful things,' said Lacey Shoestring.

'No one can hate wellington boots!' said Lauren Kelly, snapping out of her TV outro trance.

'No laces, right?' said Millie Monday.

'Exactly,' added Lacey Shoestring. 'Speaking of which ...'

Mind Bender took a step forward and tripped over. Lacey Shoestring had struck again.

'Incredible work, Lacey. Is there nothing your power of tying shoelaces can't achieve? Another supervillain captured!' said Arctic Thunder, putting his arm around her.

'I'm on the ground, but I'm not exactly captured, am I?' said Mind Bender, getting to his knees. 'Although it would appear to me that you are all captured.'

The superheroes laughed. They had all been thrown into cells and captured over the years, but standing in front of an unarmed supervillain on his knees hardly made them feel captured.

'You walked straight into my invisible cage,' said Mind Bender. 'Once inside, you can't move a single muscle in your body.'

The superheroes tried to laugh again, but it came out in a weird distorted mumble.

'Actually, that's not strictly true. You can move your mouths,' Mind Bender decided.

'You won't get away with this,' said Arctic Thunder.

'And your arms.'

'HA HA! Big mistake!' said Arctic Thunder, a little bit of lightning shooting up his arms to his fingertips.

'Only so that you can slap yourself in

the face with that wellington boot.' The lightning disappeared and Arctic Thunder picked up the boot and slapped himself in the face. Repeatedly.

WALLOP!

Despite the awful situation they were in, Millie Monday let out the faintest of giggles.

'Well, that was easy.' Mind Bender laughed. 'I wonder who will next arrive from Superhero HQ to try, and fail, to save the day ...'

CHAPTER 6

METAPHORICAL BOX

Dylan slumped down on to the bean bag in his office, his bum crashing through and hitting the hard floor beneath it. He knew the iguanas had been removing the little white balls inside over time to have fake snow fights, and they had taken so many he was now sitting on practically an empty sack. He didn't have the energy to tell them off.

The iguanas sat next to him, and the rest of the CITD sat cross-legged on the floor. Red-Eye had a bunch of the white polystyrene balls from the bean bag in his hand. Pauline shook her head, warning him against starting a fight.

'Give me a little credit,' he whispered quietly, proceeding to eat the balls as if they were popcorn. 'I can see the kid is in a bad place ...'

'So, El Capitano, that means captain in ... I want to say German? Anyway, our fearless leader, Iguana Boy, what's the plan?' said VentriloChris, unable to read the room before talking as per usual.

'The plan?' said Dylan wearily. 'There is no plan. Once again, we have been overlooked for an important supervillain mission in favour of my stupid brother and sister, and you know what, I don't blame Ron Strongman.' Dylan pulled out the rolled-up *London Bugle* from his back pocket, unravelled it and slapped the front cover.

'FAKE NEWS!'
screamed Terrifying Suzanne.

'I wish it was, but it's not. We messed up. Again. We haven't successfully brought in a supervillain since ...' Dylan cast his mind back. It was a VERY long time. If you discounted Repeat Offender as he was now a superhero, then the last time, the ONLY time, was the Platypus Kid.

'Chin up, Iguana Boy, we're only ever one mission away from turning that bad headline into a rad headline,' said VentriloChris, sticking both thumbs up.

Dylan was feeling too downhearted to respond.

'I hate to say this but VentriloChris is right,' said Paul, gesturing towards the rest of the CITD. 'We'll turn this around. But in order to do it, we need YOU to be a leader.' Dylan looked at his team, then down at the paper showing images of them performing at their worst. Paul was right. He was their leader, and it was his job, no, DUTY, to inspire them.

Dylan stood up, brushed the dust off the front of his trousers and cleared his throat.

'Friends. No ... Esteemed colleagues. Nope ... Fellow superheroes ... Members of the CITD, I want you to hear these words. I want you to really listen, box them up and keep them with you at all times, for what I am about to say is VERY important.'

'He has no idea where he's going with this, does he?' said Pauline. The iguanas shook their heads. Paul turned away, seemingly unable to watch.

'Some people think that we are useless. Others think we don't deserve to be called superheroes.'

'Got it, chief. I've taken those words

and boxed them up as requested,' said VentriloChris.

'No, not those words …' said Dylan, rubbing his eyes.

'Gotcha, removing those words from the box, and throwing the box away.'

'No, look, don't throw the box away, it's a metaphorical box …'

'Reading you loud and clear. Retrieving the metaphorical box from the bin, ready to insert your words of wisdom.'

Dylan paused, before continuing.

'I guess what I want you to know is that if nothing else, I believe in you. Every single one of you. Terrifying Suzanne, you strike fear into every supervillain that we meet.

Telepathy Twins, you don't say a lot, but when you do, it's always great to hear your valuable input ...'

'*She never shuts up,*' said Iffi.

'*Hey, you're the chatterbox in the family!*' replied Fifi.

Dylan remained oblivious to this conversation and continued. 'VentriloChris, you talk A LOT, but you keep everyone's spirits up with your positivity.'

'Thanks, Iguana Boy. You know, that reminds me of—'

'And these little guys,' said Dylan, ensuring VentriloChris didn't completely derail his inspiring speech, 'well, you don't get to hear them, but I assure you I would only be half

the leader I am without them.'

'Ah, thanks, kid,' said Paul, turning back to face him.

'Not many people see what I see, but I believe that we can overcome any obstacle, and if we all put in 110 per cent, we will be the best and most valuable team in the whole of the Superhero Collective.'

The CITD broke into a wild round of applause, and a single tear fell down the cheek of VentriloChris, who was clearly moved by the words. At this moment, Ron Strongman popped his head into the room.

'Ah yes, no need to applaud when I enter a room, settle down now. Excellent news, your brother and sister have been captured by Mind Bender.'

'How is that excellent news?' asked Dylan.

'Because we get to go and save them!?!' said Smelly Paul, clapping hysterically. Dylan hadn't thought about it like that.

'Did I say excellent? Ah well, of course I meant terrible news, yes, yes. However, it does give an opportunity to another group of heroes. Perhaps looking to prove themselves ...'

'Sounds like a great idea, sir,' said Dylan with a smile.

'Absolutely, and the excellent news is that I've sent more superheroes over now to save the day.'

'Oh,' said Dylan, who had wrongly

assumed it was going to be their shot at redemption.

'Now why did I swing by here ... ah yes, of course! There's a cat stuck in a tree in Richmond Park.'

'Right, what's the brief?' asked Dylan.

'Ah yes, well, you see, it's a tricky situation. There is a tree.'

'Right.'

'Right. And in this tree there is a cat.'

'OK ...'

'OK. And, you see, the cat is finding it a tad difficult getting out of the tree.'

'So there is a cat stuck in a tree?'

'BINGO! I knew I'd come to the right place.' Ron Strongman looked at the door where it said in big bold letters 'Cats In Trees Department', tapped it gently and chuckled.

'We won't let you down, sir,' said Dylan, feeling utterly deflated.

'Good lad, yes.' Ron Strongman nodded his head and left the room.

'Did you manage to capture all of those words in your box, because I missed quite a few of them,' said VentriloChris.

Dylan sighed, put on his cape, picked up his rucksack with the iguanas now inside it and headed towards Richmond Park, the CITD following closely behind.

CHAPTER 7

THE PHANTOM FARTER

The smell hit Dylan like a freight train as he entered the park. It was truly awful. Even Smelly Paul was holding his nose. It was the first time in Smelly Paul's life he had come across anything that smelt worse than himself.

'Wow, what is that stench?!?' said Paul.

'I never thought I'd smell anything as bad as you, Smelly Paul. No offence,' added Red-Eye.

'Offence taken! Being smelly is my thing. What am I without it?'

'Paul?' said Pauline.

'Urgh, who would want to be known as "Paul"?' said Smelly Paul.

'You know Paul is your actual name, and Smelly isn't exactly a "good" nickname to be known by,' said Paul.

'Hey, Iguana Boy.' VentriloChris's voice came out of nowhere and felt like it was practically inside Dylan's head, which made him jump.

'How many times, don't do that!' Dylan

looked around to confront VentriloChris but he couldn't see him. 'Wait a minute, where are you?'

'I'm in a lovely little coffee place, just outside the park. It smells divine in here, of warm chocolate and coffee!'

'And why aren't you here with me?'

'Because it stinks. What's going on, is there some kind of ostrich farm in the middle of the park?'

'I don't know, but something fishy is going on,' said Dylan, holding his nose.

'It smelt more trumpy than fishy to me, like rotting eggs. Anyway, I'm sure you can get the cat out of its tree without my help so I thought I would provide you with words of encouragement on this mission. From afar. Oh … you're the best.'

'Where are the rest of the CITD?'

'We're with VentriloChris,' said Iffi. This really made Dylan jump. He was (semi) used to VentriloChris's voice popping up all over the place, but this was the first time he had heard Iffi. In fact it was rare to hear her speak out loud at all.

Dylan now realised they were speaking through the headsets.

'And what about Terrifying Suzanne, surely she isn't …'

'I SAID I WANT A HAZELNUT LATTE WITH ALMOND MILK NOT REGULAR, YOU FOOL!'

'Well, I guess that answers that question.'

'It smells really bad in the park. Sorry, buddy, but good luck!' VentriloChris had sent his voice over to Dylan that last time, and then there was radio silence.

'Right, where is this stupid cat?' said Dylan, walking towards a large group of trees just inside the entrance. With every step they took deeper into the park, the smell got worse and worse.

'Honestly, what is that awful smell?!' said Paul, who had buried his nose into Dylan's jumper.

'What has this cat been eating?!' asked Pauline.

'I don't know, but whatever it is, I want the

recipe,' said Smelly Paul, who was inhaling deeply.

They reached the bottom of a tree where they found a black and white tabby cat frantically digging a hole in the ground. Once it was deep enough, the cat popped its head inside.

'Must be trying to escape the stench, poor little fella,' said Pauline.

'Like an ostrich!' added Red-Eye.

Dylan looked up at the tree, where he could see a branch mid-way up covered in scratch marks.

'Looks like this is the tree, so that must be our cat,' said Dylan, looking around for any signs of life in the park. There was nothing.

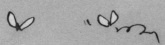

'WE DID IT!' screamed Red-Eye, letting go of holding his nose to break into a dance, something he instantly regretted.

'Looks like they were so sick of the smell they decided to risk the jump,' said Paul, playing detective.

'Looks that way. What's that over there?' Behind the trees, Dylan could just about make out a bunch of blankets and picnic baskets, all abandoned. And beyond that was a thick green fog.

'That doesn't look good at all,' said Pauline.

'It must be the Phantom Farter,' said Smelly Paul, drawing a deep breath of the foul air.

Paul gagged.

'Who is *that*?' asked Dylan, intrigued.

'Until today, I thought he was only a myth. A supervillain who creates the most obscene and vulgar stench you can dream of. The legend goes he has never been seen, only a thick green fog and the trail of destruction left in its wake. Enough of that Fart Fog in the air can turn bricks to ash and cause houses to fall down. And of course there is always THAT smell that lingers, and lingers, and lingers …'

'Then we can't stand idly by …' said Dylan, walking towards the thick green fog.

It wasn't hard to locate the whereabouts of the Phantom Farter. They simply had to follow the fog. On their way they saw dozens more abandoned picnics that had been overrun by flies and ants who seemed to be having the time of their lives.

As they moved deeper into the park, closer to the location of the Phantom Farter, the stench became fouler, more rotten, and the fog became denser. A thick cloudy haze had formed, making it impossible to see one foot in front of the other.

'Extraordinary,' said Smelly Paul wistfully. Suddenly he was in his element. He drew in another big lungful of the grotesque smog.

'What is Fart Fog?' asked Dylan in a nasal voice, struggling to breathe.

'It's a fart so perfect, so pure, that it comes out in a dense fog. In its own way, it's sort of beautiful, don't you think?' added Smelly Paul dreamily.

'No. It's disgusting,' said Paul. The others nodded, but Smelly Paul didn't seem to hear them.

The ground rumbled beneath them, and what sounded like a volcanic eruption sent them flying to the floor. It was followed by a shrill scream and a cry of

'URRRGH, GROSS!'

Dylan looked up as the fog began to clear. 'The eye of the storm,' said Smelly Paul. As the dense fog parted, they saw the Phantom Farter, bending over a picnic basket. He lifted the lid, let out another eruption, closed the lid and giggled to himself.

'Stop right there!' said Dylan, one hand on his hip, the other holding his nose. The Phantom Farter turned to face him.

'Oh hey, Iguana Boy!' he said, waving in his direction. This seemed to waft his latest fart towards Dylan, who was forced to hold his nose even tighter.

'Aaaand that's me done,' said Paul. The iguanas retreated into Dylan's bag, apart from Smelly Paul who stood triumphantly on his shoulder.

'I have so much I can learn from you,' said Smelly Paul, looking longingly at the Phantom Farter.

'Don't tell me they sent YOU to stop me?' said the Phantom Farter with a huge grin on his face. He leant to the side and squeezed out a rotten air fizzler in defiance. Dylan decided not to mention that they hadn't been sent to capture him, that they just happened to be passing by.

'I'm taking you in to Superhero HQ!' announced Dylan, still unable to take his hand from his nose. 'Your days of—'

 PARP.

'I said, your days of far—'

TOOT.

'Stop that!' said Dylan.

'Stop what?'

'You know exactly—'

FUZZY WUZZLER.

'How does he do it? Such consistency, such control ...' said Smelly Paul.

'Stop provoking him!' said Paul.

'Yeah, the smell is seeping into the bag,' added Pauline.

'I say throw in the towel. All good things have to come to an end some time, don't they, kid?' said Red-Eye.

Dylan took a step forward, then another. With each step the smell got worse and the

Fart Fog grew thicker. The Phantom Farter let out a series of farts that sounded like a popcorn machine going off, and the Fart Fog became so dense, Dylan couldn't see his own hands in front of him.

He could sense the Phantom Farter just in front of him, so he reached out his hand and lunged forwards, but there was no one there. He tripped on a loose branch and thundered to the ground.

The Fart Fog cleared once more, and there, looming over him as he lay helpless on his back, was the Phantom Farter. He stood with one leg either side of Dylan's head, an evil grin forming on his face.

'You know, I have never actually done

this before. I've always been too afraid of what might happen, but as you said you were going to turn me in to the Superhero Collective, I feel you've left me no choice …'

The Phantom Farter began to lower his bum towards Dylan's face. Smelly Paul was lying next to his head.

'It's so beautiful,' he said.

The Phantom Farter clenched his fists and gritted his teeth, and his bum began to tremble. Then, just before he was set to release a rotten air fizzler directly on to Dylan's face, he went flying across the ground.

He let out a little yelp, and sat bolt upright, looking around for the perpetrator, but there was no one there.

'Who did that?' he said.

Dylan managed to get up, but Smelly Paul continued to lie on the ground.

'What's happening?' asked Pauline.

'We were so close to experiencing the perfect fart, cheek to cheek, and it was ripped away from us!' said Smelly Paul in a sulk.

The Phantom Farter tried to stand up, but no sooner had he reached his feet than he was sent flying back on to his bum.

'Hey, stop that!' he screamed.

But each time he got up, the same thing would happen.

'I'm warning you ...' he said, clearly getting frustrated. 'If you think Fart Fog is bad, wait until I let out a Fart Explosion. If you push me one more—'

He landed plumb on his bum once more. He let out a growl of frustration and clenched his fists. He gritted his teeth, and Dylan could see the vein on his temple pulsating.

He got to his feet one last time and just as he was about to push out an almighty

PARP!!

Fart Explosion, he was down
on the ground once more,
landing on his bum at the
exact moment that the fart was
released, and he was launched
ten metres into the air.

He flew up past the tallest tree, out of the fog, and breathed fresh air for the first time in years. It made him feel sick to his belly. He then came crashing down and landed in a dainty heap in front of Dylan.

As the fog cleared, Dylan felt a light breeze on his neck, and he heard a faint whisper … 'Believe in yourself …' Then it was gone. The fog cleared, and slowly, the air became breathable again. The iguanas emerged from the bag to see Dylan standing over the Phantom Farter. A little while later they were joined by the rest of the CITD.

'What just happened?' asked Dylan, looking around him for an answer but finding nothing.

'It looks like you just captured the Phantom Farter!' said Paul.

Everyone cheered.

CHAPTER 8

SUPERHERO ZOO

The BIGGEST and BEST and most SUPER-AWESOME and OTHER WORDS THAT MAKE HIM SOUND COOL supervillain the world has ever seen was feeling a little irritated. He hadn't heard from the Prime Minister in over a week and was eager to find out what

kind of progress they had been making on his awesome new toothbrush.

'Lauren, dear,' said Mind Bender, before slapping his thigh in frustration. 'Now you've got me saying "dear".'

'Sorry, dear,' said Lauren Kelly, who was sat on the sofa polishing a wellington boot.

'I haven't heard from that wretched Prime Minister in over a week now. Can you please get in touch with her, just after I've had a chance to do my hair and wash my face ...'

'Putting you through now, dear.'

Mind Bender quickly ruffled his hair and wiped his mouth with his sleeve, appearing to be a picture of calmness as the video call connected. Before he had even had a chance to speak, the Prime Minister jumped to her defence. It seemed she had been expecting his call, he thought.

'The scientists have been working tirelessly, Mind Bender, they haven't slept in days and—'

'Yes, I'm sure they have. Do you have anything to show me, Prime Minister?'

'We do, it's just it's not ready yet …'

'Show me what you have,' he replied forcefully. The Prime Minister nodded. She picked up what looked like an ordinary toothbrush.

'Now, this may look like an ordinary toothbrush,' she said, holding it up to the camera.

'Yes, it does. Also, it's not golden.'

'Quite correct, we are still working on that. Now look what happens when I press this button.' The Prime Minister pressed the button and the electric toothbrush began to vibrate. Mind Bender said nothing.

'It turns on,' said the Deputy Prime Minister, filling the void of silence. Mind Bender took a deep breath and motioned for them to continue with his hand.

'Now, here is the really cool bit ...' The Prime Minister beckoned the cameraman forward, and they moved to the back of the room, to a balcony that overlooked a huge warehouse. The cameraman leaned over the side and zoomed in on a fancy-looking golden plane.

'Isn't that cool? Gold too!' she said.

'That does look pretty cool. How fast does it fly?' asked Mind Bender, excited about the prospect of queues at the airport fading into a distant memory and long-haul flights being a thing of the past.

'It's the fastest plane in the sky. We managed to get to Tenerife in a little over an hour.'

'An HOUR?!' roared Mind Bender. 'TENERIFE?!?' he continued. 'I was very specific: less than forty-five seconds to ANYWHERE in the world.' That was NOT going to get him to Sydney, Australia. It simply wasn't good enough.

'Ah yes, well, we are still working on that aspect, and the whole turning the toothbrush into the plane bit too. Other than that, we are making good progress.'

'Good progress? What part of any of this would you describe as good progress?'

The Prime Minister was visibly sweating now; she nodded her head to the side, looking off camera. The cameraman swung round to show a scientist holding a golden toothbrush in one hand and a can of gold spray paint in the other.

'Golden toothbrush, tick,' said the Prime Minister, ticking the air with her finger and forcing a smile through gritted teeth.

'That's not good enough!' screamed Mind

Bender, clearly frustrated by the lack of progress.

'Look, Mind Bender, I'm sorry to say this, I really am, but I just don't think what you are asking for is possible,' said the Deputy Prime Minister.

'But it's what I want, and I ALWAYS get what I want!' said Mind Bender.

'Yes, I understand that, I watched *Strictly Come Prancing*, with the horses – very good by the way, I still can't believe Golden Star didn't win – but your demand for a golden toothbrush that will fly you around the world is simply impossible.'

'Let me tell you something, Deputy Prime Minister, people don't say NO to ME. Come here, you guys.'

Mind Bender gestured off camera, beckoning someone over to the sofa. At the bottom of the screen, the Deputy Prime Minister noticed two people crawling into view. It was Arctic Thunder and Millie Monday.

Millie jumped up on to the sofa and was panting like a dog. She then began to bark. Arctic Thunder remained on all fours in front of the camera, his head bowed, every now and again raising it to look around.

Atomic Adam then jumped up from behind the sofa, thumping his chest and screeching. He began picking through Millie's hair as if he was looking for fleas. Lacey Shoestring crawled on to the back of the sofa. From a bag she took out a blue jumper that almost matched the colour of Lauren Kelly's sofa. She put it on and licked her lips.

'See, Prime Minister, she's a chameleon. Pretty clever, huh? I just told her to act like a lizard, and she went and found all the extra clothes in the wardrobe department. I must say, even I was impressed.'

In the background, even more superheroes were larking about, flapping their arms and cawing as if they were a group of migrating birds.

'By the way, you might want to get a message to Ron Strongman to stop sending superheroes to try and stop me, as none of them have even got close to capturing me. On second thoughts, tell him to carry on. I will just add them to my growing collection of zoo animals.'

He had captured a second wave of superheroes that morning. Mind Bender looked behind him and chuckled as he saw a few superheroes crash into each other as they flew around aimlessly.

'The point is, no one says no to me, not even the world's most powerful superheroes. If I say jump ...'

'We say "how high?",' said the Deputy Prime Minister, finally understanding the gravity of the situation.

147

'NO! You just jump. You don't ask me any questions. You just do it. Understand?'

'Yes, Mind Bender,' said the Deputy Prime Minister, skulking to the back of the room.

'Sorry about that, Mind Bender, of course we will get your plane to you, very soon, I promise,' said the Prime Minister, her eyes seemingly pleading for forgiveness.

'You have one week. Then there will be consequences for your continued failure.' Mind Bender approached the camera. 'I'll leave you with this. If I can turn superheroes into zoo attractions, think about what I could do to you and your government, Prime Minister ...'

Arctic Thunder looked directly at the

camera and let out a piercing

'HIIIIISSSSSSSSSSSSSSS'.

The screen went off.

'Good job, everyone, now back in your cage, please.' The superheroes went back to their invisible cages, where they instantly found themselves stuck.

Mind Bender chuckled. 'Tenerife ... Sydney, Australia, I'll be seeing you soon ...'

CHAPTER 9

BACK IN THE GOOD BOOKS

When Dylan and the rest of the CITD made it back to Superhero HQ they weren't exactly met with a hero's welcome. Or any welcome at all in fact.

'Uhm ... where is everyone?' said Paul, looking around the vast empty reception hall. It was eerily silent and then they heard

the rapid pitter-patter of frantic footsteps approaching.

'I can't be late ... I can't be late ...' said a rather worried-looking superhero as he flashed past them. Dylan and VentriloChris looked at each other. 'Briefing room,' they said in unison. They all ran in the direction of the briefing room.

Dylan had been late to a Ron Strongman briefing before and didn't want to be in that position again.

When they entered, they saw the frantic-looking hero who had run past them, panting heavily in the front row. He was joined by a handful of other superheroes who filled a few seats in the two front rows.

'Uh, where is everyone else?' asked Paul.

'No idea. Quick, let's take a seat before Ron Strongman gets here.' Dylan headed straight to the front row and sat down in the first empty seat he could find.

'Long time no see, Iguana Boy,' said the superhero in the next seat.

'Zac!' said Dylan excitedly before quickly correcting himself. 'I mean, the Outtatime Kid ... *sorry*,' he whispered, having accidentally said his real name out loud. No one seemed to notice and the Outtatime Kid didn't appear to mind. In fact he was smiling even more than when Dylan had first sat down.

'Don't apologise, *never* apologise to me. I

owe you everything. You can sing my name from the rooftops for all I care.'

'I could do that for you now, if you like. Throw my voice up to the rooftops, although I'm not the greatest singer. Besides, you should really be careful about your secret identity,' said VentriloChris. The Outtatime Kid continued to smile.

'Good to see you too, VentriloChris. Good to see all of you.' He waved towards the rest of the CITD who had helped fill out the front row. Iffi and Fifi waved back and Terrifying Suzanne blushed. The Outtatime Kid was kind of a big deal at Superhero HQ these days.

'Where have you been? We haven't seen

you in ages,' said Dylan.

'Off saving the world mostly, and I mean *the world*. Mr Strongman put me in charge of International Relations, so I'm often visiting other countries, helping out their superheroes.'

'That's so cool. I'm glad to hear it.' And Dylan really meant it. Although he was often jealous of his brother and sister and their success, he was genuinely happy to see the Outtatime Kid doing so well, having played a vital role in helping him become a superhero.

'What are you doing back here, Outtatime?'

'Not sure; Mr Strongman asked me to come back urgently. Didn't say why.'

'Ah yes, quieten down now, everybody,' said Ron, not looking up from the remote control he had in his hands as he wandered on stage. He walked into the mic stand and knocked it over. He then looked up to see the handful of superheroes in front of him. Usually, the entire room would have been filled. 'Yes, well, let us begin.'

'He's going to start the briefing? Hardly anyone is here!' The Outtatime Kid shrugged his shoulders and faced forward.

'Now, unfortunately another band of superheroes have been captured in our latest attempts to bring down the supervillain known as Mind Bender. Yes, yes, it is rather unfortunate. The latest government interaction is quite worrying, quite worrying indeed ...'

Ron pressed play on the remote and the screen showed the Government's frantic attempts to please Mind Bender, followed by what seemed like half of Superhero HQ acting like wild animals.

Everyone in the briefing room had concern written all over their faces, except for the members of the CITD who were fighting back laughter as they watched Arctic Thunder and Millie Monday making fools of themselves. When Arctic hissed at the end of the clip, Dylan cried with laughter. Luckily Ron Strongman misread Dylan's feelings.

'Yes, yes, I know. It's truly horrible to

see, I'm close to tears myself. Now, I know that we are down to the bare bones at the moment, what with half our team clucking, cawing and chirping and failing to capture Mind Bender, but I wanted to take a few seconds to congratulate Iguana Boy and the CITD.'

Dylan suddenly sat bolt upright and pointed towards himself in surprise. Ron Strongman nodded.

'Yes, you see, Iguana Boy managed to capture the elusive Phantom Farter this morning, a supervillain who has long fallen under our radar. Excellent job, truly excellent.'

Dylan smiled as he heard his hero talking

about him in front of the entire Superhero Collective. Well, maybe not the entire, more like half. Under half in fact. At least in front of SOME other superheroes, anyway. However, the smile lasted only the briefest of moments as he thought back to the morning's events.

He hadn't done anything and neither had anyone in his team. Some mysterious hero had swooped in, saved the day and then swooped out. In fact, he wasn't sure they had swooped – after all, he hadn't been able to see them.

A small round of applause rippled around the room, mostly led by the Outtatime Kid who once more was positively beaming.

'Now, on to the important matter at hand. Bringing Mind Bender to justice. In light of what I have seen this morning, there is only one person I can ask to put this matter firmly to bed ...'

'This is it, kid, your big chance!' said Paul.

'And that person is ...'

'IGUANA BOY!' shouted Red-Eye.

'The Outtatime Kid, who I am happy to say is back here in London to help us out.'

Ron clapped vigorously and motioned for him to join him on stage. The Outtatime Kid looked painfully at Dylan and mouthed the word 'sorry' as he went up on stage. He knew how much taking down a big supervillain meant to Dylan.

The briefing ended, and as everyone was leaving the room, Ron Strongman leaped off the stage and put his arm around Dylan.

'Excellent work today, Iguana Boy, excellent, excellent work.' Dylan forced a smile. 'I have another mission for you, or two in fact. No wait, perhaps even three, it's getting a little thin on the ground around here, in case you hadn't noticed. Plenty of superhero work to do!' Ron patted him on the back and left Dylan and the CITD alone in the briefing room.

'That's brilliant, looks like we are back in his good books!' said VentriloChris.

'One or two, or three missions coming our way. That's pretty exciting!' said Pauline.

'Yeah, only we really don't deserve them,' said Dylan.

'What do you mean? We just brought in a legendary supervillain!' said VentriloChris.

'Did we? None of you were there, you lot were in a coffee shop, and we had nothing to do with it. Some invisible hero turned up and did all the work for us.'

'Chin up, Iguana Boy. Bad people are off the streets and we have gotten a second chance to prove ourselves as superheroes.'

'I suppose so,' said Dylan, thinking about their situation. His first instinct had been to tell Ron Strongman what had happened, but VentriloChris was making a good point. A supervillain was off the streets and they could go back out into the world to do some good. On reflection, he could live with that.

'You're right!' said Dylan, picking himself up. 'This is our chance to redeem ourselves. Let's head back out into this crazy city and get ourselves on a mission or two.'

'Or three!' added VentriloChris.

$$\text{CHAPTER 10}$$

TWINKLE TWINKLE LITTLE BAAAAA

The BIGGEST and BEST and most SUPER-AWESOME and OTHER WORDS THAT MAKE HIM SOUND COOL supervillain the world has ever seen was enjoying having an army of superheroes at his disposal. Not that he was plotting to use them to do anything in particular, he just found having

them around rather entertaining.

Most supervillains would give their right arm for an army of superheroes. They would stay up all night plotting and conspiring over all the dastardly things they could do to ultimately take over the entire world. However, Mind Bender wasn't your average supervillain. He didn't really have any idea what he wanted, which is why he ended up asking the Prime Minister for a toothbrush.

Although that isn't strictly true. He did have SOME idea about what he wanted. He wanted to be entertained, and a room full of superheroes with a vast array of different superpowers, who would do ANYTHING you tell them: now, that could provide years of fun!

Mind Bender had lined up the superheroes inside the warehouse and was standing in front of them holding a wellington boot.

He cleared his throat, and then counted down from three, before pointing the welly at Arctic Thunder who hissed. Then he pointed it at Millie Monday, who barked, and Lacey Shoestring, who cawed. As he pointed at each superhero, they made their animal sound, in a certain octave that allowed Mind Bender to create a tune. They were hissing, barking and cawing the tune of 'Twinkle Twinkle Little Star' (or the alphabet song, which has the EXACT same tune. This had blown his mind when he had discovered this fact …).

Mind Bender was just about to reach the end of the song; he had just a few notes to go, the notes for 'what you are'. He pointed at Arctic Thunder.

'Hiss, hiss …'

'BAAAAA,' said the Outtatime Kid, who to the complete and utter surprise of Mind Bender had entered the warehouse on all fours and baaaed the last note of the song.

'Uhm … OK, well I guess you're captured too. Weird, I didn't even have to do anything!'

Of course, the Outtatime Kid had the ability to turn back time by thirty seconds, and this is what had *actually* happened …

THIRTY SECONDS AGO

'Hiss, hiss...'

'You're coming with me, Mind Bender,' said the Outtatime Kid.

'Oh it's you, the kid who can turn back time. FREEZE!' said Mind Bender, causing the Outtatime Kid to freeze instantly. 'Oh, this could be fun ... I want you to turn back time and when you come back, I want you to be a sheep! That is going to confuse the life out of me, how fun!'

BACK TO THE PRESENT

'OK, so I've been thinking about what we could do, you know, for a bit of fun, and I think I've finally got it!' said Mind Bender, hardly able to contain his excitement. 'Superhero Olympics! Right here, in this TV studio!' None of the superheroes responded; they all stared blankly into space. 'All of you cheer uncontrollably.' The superheroes whooped and clapped and cheered uncontrollably.

'So we are going to have to use the things we see around us as we don't exactly have all the equipment they have at the real Olympics,' said Mind Bender, surveying the room. 'Of course! Our first event will be Welly Throwing!'

Mind Bender set up the room, putting a huge number of wellies at the far end of the studio and marking out the floor at intervals of three metres. Well, *he* didn't do it, Lauren Kelly did, but he made her do it so it's pretty much the same thing.

'Ladies and superheroes ... wait, that isn't right ... Ladies and gentlemen and superheroes ... nope ... Superheroes, we are gathered here today to witness the birth of ... No!'

Mind Bender was getting frustrated by his opening ceremony speech. He asked the Outtatime Kid to reverse time so he could get it right. After about an hour he ended up with, 'Welcome to the Superhero Olympics: let the games begin!'

What Mind Bender hadn't counted on is just how competitive superheroes are. Up

169

first was Millie Monday, who was only a superhero on Mondays. Today was Tuesday so she managed to somehow throw the boot backwards.

'Not the best start!' said Mind Bender, laughing.

Next up to throw his welly was Liquid, a superhero with the ability to breathe underwater. This wasn't particularly useful for throwing a welly, but he was muscly so he managed a reasonable six metres. He seemed pretty happy.

Then came Arctic Thunder, who managed seven metres, and this is where things started to get a little out of hand, as Liquid was certain the welly had only got further than his due to 'wind assistance'. Arctic Thunder denied this categorically, with a huge smile on his face.

That smile soon faded, though, as the Outtatime Kid threw the boot an impressive distance of eight metres. Arctic Thunder looked on miserably, muttering under his breath that the Outtatime Kid must have had multiple goes because of his time-rewinding abilities and that it wasn't fair.

Finally, up stepped Atomic Adam, who threw the welly a meagre five metres across the floor. He was so angry that he threw down a huge ball of belly button fluff which exploded and his boot launched high into the air, landing a full fifteen metres away from

them. Atomic Adam immediately started celebrating, but everyone got so irritated they began fighting each other. For a second, Mind Bender became cautious, worried it might be a classic superhero ruse to attack him. But then he remembered he had told them with his power of persuasion not to bother trying to escape and he relaxed.

The Superhero Olympics were over before they had even really begun.

Mind Bender looked on at the superhero fight in front of him and chuckled. *It really is one heck of a fight*, he thought.

'Superheroes, listen up,' he said. 'When I head over to Sydney, Australia I'm taking you all with me – you're just

TOO MUCH FUN!'

CHAPTER 11

THE INVISIBLE SUPERHERO

Everything was suddenly going well for the CITD; they were being given more and more missions, as more and more superheroes were taken hostage by Mind Bender. This meant that they were taking down supervillain after supervillain, keeping the streets of London safe, and in the process, getting heaps and

heaps of praise from Ron Strongman.

Only there was one teeny little problem: they weren't doing ANY of the superhero work ...

Yes, the Invisible Hero seemed to be following the CITD wherever they went. Dylan was comfortable taking the credit for the Phantom Farter in order to get his career back on track, but doing it over and over again ... well, it made Dylan feel sick.

Of course, he was happy that supervillains were being taken off the streets, but he wanted to be a superhero so he could help people, and standing around watching another superhero do all the work didn't seem right. Especially as he had done that for years before getting his powers, watching his brother and sister save the day over and over again.

The hardest part, though, was taking the

credit. After all, the mysterious superhero who had been helping them out was completely invisible. The invisible hero would swoop in (usually just as the CITD were about to mess up), casually save the day and then swoop out again. So far, Dylan hadn't had one interaction with them.

The CITD's latest mission saw them taking on a fearsome supervillain who could throw fireballs from their hands. Normally Dylan would approach such a dangerous mission with extreme caution, but knowing he wouldn't have to do any superhero work at all, he paid very little attention to what was going on.

'Soon I will take over the world!' said Fire

Fist, bright red flames emerging from his clenched fists.

'Sure, buddy, sure ...' said Dylan. Moments later, Fire Fist was on the floor, and a rope magically wrapped around him and tied itself in a knot.

'YES!' screamed VentriloChris, punching the air. 'CITD to the rescue AGAIN!' Dylan sighed.

'What's wrong, Dylan, you OK?'

'Yet again, we are taking credit for capturing a supervillain when we did absolutely nothing,' he said wearily.

'You know, you could always let me go if you like. Catch me yourself?' said the supervillain, Fire Fist, whimpering.

Dylan ignored him and marched over to the police officer who had just arrived on the scene.

'Thank you, Iguana Boy. I don't know what this city would do without the CITD!' said the police officer, smiling at Dylan. The police officer wasn't concentrating on what he was doing and he banged the supervillain's head on the roof as he lowered him into the car.

'Don't mention it,' said Dylan. He wasn't being polite, he really meant it – he really didn't want him to mention it.

The rest of the CITD were all high-fiving each other, celebrating another successful mission. Even the iguanas were getting involved, all except Red-Eye who was high-fiving the air above his head aimlessly.

'What are you doing?' asked Smelly Paul.

'I'm trying to high-five the Invisible Hero!' said Red-Eye. Dylan turned away and walked off without saying a word.

'BOOM! Got her! I think ...' said Red-Eye.

After the mission, the CITD returned to their office. Dylan was quiet while the rest of the team celebrated yet another successful capture of a supervillain. He looked at them in amazement, unsure of how they could be so happy taking the credit. 'How can any of you be happy with this mysterious superhero doing all the work?'

'Easy, they are not mysterious,' said VentriloChris. 'You see, I've given them a name. The Invisible Superhero. Now they are part of the gang, one of the CITD. We win together, we lose together!'

'THAT IS STUPID!' screamed Terrifying Suzanne.

'You do crack me up, Suzie T,' said VentriloChris.

'She's right, that is stupid,' said Fifi.

'Yeah, the Invisible Superhero, what a rubbish name! They should be called something cool like Myst. You know, because they are mysterious and you can't

see them, like mist,' said Iffi, feeling pretty proud of herself.

'But you *can* see mist,' said Fifi.

'Here we go,' said Pauline, who had seen the Telepathy Twins argue on several occasions. She much preferred it when they did it in their own heads, but this one was out loud for everyone to hear.

'No you can't, it's see-through.'

'Yes, you can see through it, but it doesn't make it see-*through*. I can see through a window, but I can also see the window.'

'They are not going to be called Window. That's a stupid superhero name.'

'I wasn't suggesting they were called Window, but now you mention it, it's a

better name than Myst …' They began
pushing each other back and forth with their
foreheads.

'No it's not.'

'Yes it is.'

'No it's not.'

'Yes it is.'

'THEY ARE CALLED INCOGNITO!!!!'

screamed Terrifying Suzanne.

'YES! Excellent name, Tezza,' said VentriloChris, offering up a high five which was declined with an evil stare.

'That works!' said Iffi, taking her weight off her sister's head and standing upright.

'Yeah, I like it,' added Fifi, doing the same.

'Then it's settled, Incognito is the newest member of the CITD and we're all awesome superheroes!' said VentriloChris.

Dylan slapped his forehead in despair. 'But we aren't doing ANYTHING! This invisible superhero—'

'Incognito!' interrupted Red-Eye, who was

184

quite fond of the name.

'Incognito, or whatever you want to call them, is doing the work. Have you ever wondered why? What if they're a double agent, looking to get closer to the Superhero Collective to bring us down?'

'I think you're clutching at straws, Iguana Boy,' said VentriloChris. 'Incognito is part of the CITD and everything we have done is a team effort.'

'What have you actually done?' said Dylan, getting up from his chair. 'What have ANY of you done in the past two months to help bring down a supervillain?' Dylan surveyed the room; they were all lost in deep thought.

'Well, this one time there was a super-evil

supervillain called the Phantom Farter and he was all like PARP, PFFFT, TRUMP, and I was all like K'POW!' said Red-Eye.

'Any of you?' said Dylan, ignoring him entirely.

'I've done LOADS of helpful stuff,' said VentriloChris triumphantly.

'OK, name one thing.'

'There was that supervillain the other day, the one with the weird eyes ...'

'Oh yeah, he was freaky-looking. A real weirdo,' said Red-Eye, picking his nose with his tail.

'When we got to the warehouse, I said, "There he is," and I stretched my arm out and extended a single finger in his direction so everyone could see him.'

'So, you pointed at him? You pointed at the only other person in the warehouse apart from us, who by that time, had already been tied up by Incognito?'

'You're welcome.'

'You're all living in a dream world. We need to start helping people again, otherwise what's the point?'

Dylan stormed out of the room. He had no idea where he was going or what he was going to do. As he paced the corridor, an overwhelming urge came over him. He couldn't fight it, he was powerless to resist. He had made up his mind. He HAD to tell Ron Strongman the truth ...

CHAPTER 12

CONFESSION

'Ah, Iguana Boy, just the superhero I wanted to see. Sit down, please, sit, sit.' Ron gestured towards a large ball that had seemingly replaced the chair opposite his desk. Dylan then noticed that Ron seemed to be bobbing up and down ever so slightly and he too was sitting on a large exercise ball.

'Apparently these are good for your core. Ruddy uncomfortable though,' said Ron, shuffling to find a comfy position unsuccessfully. 'What can I do for you?'

'Well, sir ...'

'Excellent work capturing your latest supervillain, by the way. Truly inspiring,' said Ron.

'Yes, well, that's why I'm here. You see—'

'Front-page news again, no doubt.'

'Yes, I'm sure, but you see—'

'I know what this is about,' said Ron, stopping Dylan mid-sentence once again.

'You do?' Dylan was kind of relieved. He had been wrestling with the best way of telling Ron about Incognito, but if he already knew that made things much easier.

'Yes, yes of course. You want me to tell you who is going to win next month's Superstar Award.'

'No, honestly, I would never—'

'I've seen this look before, you know. From your brother of course. I can see the same hunger in you as I did in him when he was your age.'

'We are nothing alike,' said Dylan firmly.

'Nonsense, you are very similar, both HUGE successes in the Superhero Collective! Well, slightly less of a success these days, your brother, having been captured and turned into a cow … however, I must tell you what I told him, repeatedly I might add.

I cannot let you know who is going to win the Superstar Award. It wouldn't be fair on everyone else.'

'No, I completely understand, but I really need to talk to you about—'

'OK, OK, you've twisted my arm. It's you! Of course it's you, what an excellent month you have had. Brilliant job, Iguana Boy, simply brilliant.'

'IT WASN'T ME!' screamed Dylan, frustrated at how difficult Ron was making it for him to come clean.

'You think I should give the award to someone else? Very selfless, Iguana Boy, but I have already had the trophy maker inscribe your name and it costs £1.47 per letter ...'

'No, all of the missions, the capturing of supervillains. It wasn't me. Nor was it my team. We turned up at the missions, but each time we did, someone else saved the day.' Dylan bowed his head and awaited his punishment. It didn't come; instead Ron said nothing.

Dylan continued. 'The person saving the missions has been some sort of invisible superhero. We were close to messing up each time and they saved us. We have been referring to them as "Incognito".'

Ron still said nothing.

'Sir? Did you hear what I said?'

'You know, I think you're being pretty hard on yourself, Iguana Boy,' said Ron

Strongman, bouncing his exercise ball like a space hopper around to the other side of the desk. He was now sat directly opposite Dylan. 'Did you ever think that this "mysterious hero" that *no one else can see*, is YOU?'

Dylan looked confused. 'Mr Strongman, sir, I don't understand.'

'Think about it logically for a second. Have you ever met a superhero who didn't want to be a superhero? Who goes around doing superhero stuff without being seen as a superhero?'

'Well ... no ... of course not, but ...'

'Then why hasn't this mysterious and supposedly *invisible* hero come forward?'

'I don't know,' said Dylan, mulling this over. Ron did have a point. Why was the invisible hero allowing the CITD to take all of the credit? Something didn't add up.

'Maybe … just maybe … it's you. YOU are the invisible hero and you don't even know it.'

'That doesn't make sense …'

'And an invisible hero who takes NONE of the credit does? Maybe you have developed a new power. Your sister was roasting a chicken at the kitchen table with her laser eyes when she suddenly lifted off the ground and discovered she could also fly. Your brother, too, could only make it rain at first. Maybe you are sending out an

invisible force.'

'I guess you could be right ...' said Dylan, wondering if this could possibly be true.

'You need to BELIEVE in yourself, Iguana Boy! Believe that you are the superhero you have always WANTED to be.

'And you can take your first step towards this newfound belief by bringing in the world's most wanted supervillain,' said Ron teasingly.

'You mean ...'

'Mind Bender!' Ron bounced ferociously as he said his name. Dylan joined him.

'Yeah ... YEAH,' he said louder, finding an inner confidence. 'You're right! I just need to BELIEVE in myself.'

'That's right!'

'I can do it. I can bring Mind Bender to justice!'

'Yes you can! I need you to do this for the entire Superhero Collective, Iguana Boy. We are just one PR disaster away from having to rename the Superhero Collective again and I'm running out of names. We're still scrubbing POOP off the wall from the last time we were made to look like fools.'

Dylan let out a little chuckle. Cleaning POOP off the walls, come on, who wouldn't laugh at that?!?

Dylan left Ron's office with a spring in his step and made his way back to the CITD office. When he arrived, the iguanas were playing their favourite game, launching coats using their tails from the back of the room towards the coat hooks on the far wall.

'I win again!' said Pauline smugly.

'It's not fair, tails are much more nimble than legs,' said VentriloChris, who was lying on his back with his leg in the air. There was a coat over his head; clearly he hadn't been successful in launching the coat forwards.

'I just told Ron Strongman everything. About Incognito ...'

A hush fell over the room. VentriloChris removed the coat and stood up. 'Really? Are we all fired?' he asked plainly.

'No. He gave us the Mind Bender mission.'

'That's AMAZING!' said VentriloChris, giving Dylan a huge bear hug. Everyone started celebrating.

'That's great news, but I thought you weren't comfortable with the whole Incognito thing ...' said Pauline cautiously.

'Look, forget Incognito, who knows, perhaps they don't even exist. Maybe one of US has just developed a new awesome power we are unaware of ...'

Everyone looked at each other with wide-eyed anticipation. Dylan thought this was pretty stupid, as clearly if anyone had developed a new power, it was him. He was the leader and besides, he was the one who needed it most. He could only talk to iguanas after all ...

'Are you OK, Dylan?' asked Pauline, who now seemed quite worried about him. This wasn't like Dylan at all, she thought.

'I've never been better, Pauline!'

'It just seems you may have lost your way a little ...'

'Quite the opposite, I've simply FOUND my belief. In me. In this awesome team!' Everyone started cheering, but Pauline didn't join in.

'So what's the plan, boss?' asked Iffi.

'OOOH, did someone say plan?!?' said Paul. The iguanas LOVED making plans.

'Good point, we need a plan,' said Dylan, looking around the room for someone to kick things off. 'OK, Paul, what have you got?'

'Let's see … Got it! You know how Mind Bender can get people to do anything he wants?'

'Yes, that is his power, go on,' said Dylan.

'Why don't we get him to convince HIMSELF to release the superheroes and hand himself in?' Paul gave a little bow at the end of his plan and Red-Eye cheered.

'OK, and how exactly do we do that?' asked Dylan.

'Get him to talk into a mirror maybe?'

'OK, we'll park that idea for now, but

good effort. Red-Eye, any ideas?'

'Yep.'

'Any that DON'T involve dinosaurs?'

'Nope.'

'Fair enough. Smelly Paul?'

'Uhm ... Is his supervillain hideout on an ostrich farm?'

'No,' replied Dylan.

'Oh, well, that's disappointing. Nothing from me then.'

'I have a FANTASTIC plan!' said VentriloChris, jumping into the middle of the circle the superheroes had formed. 'Step One, we head over to the warehouse where Mind Bender is keeping the superheroes hostage. You all keeping up?' Everyone

202

nodded impatiently. 'OK great, now keep with me because this is where it really steps up a notch. Step Two, we enter the building and wait for Incognito, or ONE OF US with our awesome new power we don't even know we have, to save the day. BOOM! Mic drop.' VentriloChris pretended to drop a microphone on the floor and then began clapping.

'That's not exactly a pla— You know what, good effort, VentriloChris, I'll throw that in the maybe pile too. Telepathy Twins, anything to say?'

'Well, we've actually been working really hard on a plan,' said Iffi.

'It might be the BEST plan ever made,' said

Fifi triumphantly.

'Didn't think so,' said Dylan, whose question had been greeted by utter silence.

'Terrifying S—'

'GRAB HIM AND THROW HIM IN A TINY BOX AND LOCK THE BOX AND THEN SIT ON TOP OF THE BOX!'

'Wow. Well, that's going in the maybe pile as it's the most put-together sentence I have ever heard you say, even if it is fairly disturbing.' Dylan was about to wrap things up when he suddenly realised he hadn't heard from the most sensible person in the room. Or should that be iguana … 'Pauline, you've been unusually quiet. Anything to add?'

'Yes I do. Are you SURE you're OK?'

'Actually, no,' said Dylan to the surprise of the other iguanas. 'You see, I could really use a plan right about now, and I've not heard from the best plan maker I know.' Pauline couldn't help but smile, and though she tried to resist, the temptation to throw in a plan was simply too much.

'Well, if you're sure you're OK and you want to go after Mind Bender ... uhm ... I guess I'm pretty good at throwing things ...'

'You're the BEST at throwing things!' said Red-Eye.

'Thank you.' Pauline blushed. 'And there are plenty of wellington boots around as it's the studio where they film *Kelly's Wellies*.'

'LOVE THAT SHOW!' said Red-Eye,

grabbing his foot and attempting to throw it, flipping himself over in the process.

'So I could throw a boot at his head, then we could make our escape with the superheroes?'

'Brilliant. Simple, yet effective!' said Dylan. The Telepathy Twins hoisted Dylan on to their shoulders, whilst the iguanas did the same to Pauline and paraded them around the room.

'Right, everyone, onwards to the TV studio!' exclaimed Dylan and everyone cheered.

IGUANA BOY VS MIND BENDER THE SHOWDOWN

The CITD arrived at the TV studio, ready to unleash the full fury of Pauline's plan.

'Ah man, this is going to be so good!' said Smelly Paul, rubbing his hands together excitedly.

'Yeah, you are going to launch that wellington boot and it's gonna be all like

208

K'POW! On his big stupid head!' added Red-Eye.

Dylan chuckled, and then it hit him. A wellington boot that is, not an idea. Right in his head. It was Lauren Kelly, flinging boot after boot in their direction. They had made their way into the heart of the studio and found themselves cowering behind the sofa.

'Ouch, that really hurt!' said Dylan, a bruise forming on the left side of his forehead.

'Don't worry, Dylan, we've got your back,' said VentriloChris.

'I HATE WELLINGTON BOOTS!' screamed Terrifying Suzanne.

'Time for the plan!' said Paul. The iguanas scuttled out from behind the sofa, avoiding the barrage of seemingly never-ending wellington boots. They managed to grab a boot, put it on Red-Eye's back, and transport it back to Dylan.

'With Pauline's throwing skills, we will only need one welly. Do your worst, Pauline,' said Red-Eye.

Pauline placed the wellington boot upright

and wrapped her tail around it tightly. Then she peered over the sofa to see exactly where Lauren Kelly was standing.

She hopped off, and braced herself for launch. 'One ...' She gripped the carpet underneath her feet tightly. 'Two ...' She tensed every muscle in her body and gritted her teeth. 'THREE!' She thrust her body forward, bringing her tail above her head, but the wellington boot was MUCH heavier than she had imagined, and it didn't even make it above the sofa. She let go and it slapped Dylan on the side of his face.

'OUCH!' said Dylan, who now had an almost identical mark on the right side of his forehead.

'Ooooh, you kinda look like you have devil horns,' said VentriloChris.

'Sorry, Dylan,' said Pauline.

'What do we do now without a plan?' asked Paul.

'I don't kno—'began Dylan and then, as if by magic, the boots stopped flying. Dylan cautiously peered over the top of the sofa, checking to see if Lauren Kelly was simply reloading, but instead she was stuck underneath a huge pile of her own wellington boots.

'See, keeping it simple …'

'Yet effective.' Red-Eye finished Dylan's train of thought. Once again things had worked out perfectly. This new superpower, even though he had no idea how it worked, was unstoppable.

'Right, the coast is clear, let's move forward,' said Dylan, emerging from the sofa. VentriloChris ran ahead in front of him and when he reached the far wall, he turned around dramatically and motioned for them to stop.

'Well, look who finally decided to show up. If it isn't the worst superhero EVER, Iguana Boy,' said VentriloChris, an evil grin forming on his face.

'Uh ... what did you say?' said Dylan, a little confused.

'You seriously think you can defeat me, MIND BENDER?!?' said VentriloChris, raising his arms in the air.

'I knew it!' said Red-Eye. 'VentriloChris IS Mind Bender.'

'What?!?' said the other iguanas, genuinely befuzzled by this revelation.

'These things always have a twist. It just

makes so much sense now. I mean, have you ever seen the two of them in the same room together?'

'Yes,' said Dylan, pointing towards Mind Bender, who was walking towards them accompanied by an army of superheroes, including his brother and sister.

'Oh,' said Red-Eye. Mind Bender was closer to VentriloChris than the rest of the CITD was, so Dylan couldn't hear his commands, but he could clearly see him whispering something. VentriloChris nodded and then began breakdancing. Extremely badly. He tried to do a spin on his head and collapsed in a heap on the floor.

'Try and fight it, VentriloChris; he is

controlling you. He is controlling all of
you!' said Dylan in vain to the rest of the
superheroes.

'Oooh, good idea, you should fight it,
VentriloChris,' said Mind Bender. 'See if
you can slap my control of you right out

of your head ...' VentriloChris began slapping himself.

'Ha! Brilliant. Hmmm ... what else can I do ... ?' Mind Bender took a step closer towards the CITD. He pointed to the Telepathy Twins. 'You two, get on your hands and knees.' They did what they were told without saying a word (probably). 'Now you, little terrifying girl, get on top of them.'

'THIS IS RIDICULOUS, YOU FOOL!' said Terrifying Suzanne as she climbed on top of them.

'Now let's see ... Ah, got it, this will be HILARIOUS! Arctic Thunder, create a storm, would you, and sweep that kid up into it ...' said Mind Bender, pointing at

VentriloChris, who was now curled up in a ball on the floor.

'What are you doing?' said Dylan, frozen to the spot.

'Now, throw him at the human pyramid

over there!' Arctic Thunder launched
VentriloChris towards the other members
of the CITD and they all
crashed to the floor in
a pile of defeated
superheroes.
Mind Bender
was laughing
uncontrollably
as he moved
backwards,
then suddenly
he fell,
tripping
over thin
air.

'What the ... !?!?'

'AH HA! I have you now, Mind Bender,' said Dylan triumphantly.

'Who did that?' Mind Bender returned to his feet only to feel an invisible force push him over again. 'Stop it!'

'I don't even know how I'm doing it, so how can I stop it?!' said Dylan.

'You don't know how ... Then it can't be you ... It must be a ... Reveal yourself, invisible hero!' demanded Mind Bender, and no sooner had he said this than a girl appeared out of thin air, her hair blocking her face. She was wearing a school uniform that looked incredibly familiar to Dylan. That's because he saw it every single day.

Dylan stared at the girl in total shock.

Mind Bender was also staring; he had never seen a superhero wearing a school uniform before. 'Now that's a strange costume,' he said.

'You don't really need a costume when you can turn invisible. Seemed like a waste of time trying to design one,' the girl said, getting up off the floor. She flicked back her hair and looked directly at Dylan.

'Cara?!?' he stuttered. 'CARA!?!' he exclaimed, seemingly unable to say anything else.

'Cara? That girl who stood up for you at school?' said Pauline.

'See. There's always a twist,' said Red-Eye.

'I'm sorry, Dylan, I wanted to tell you …'

'It was you, this whole time?!?'

'Uh …' she muttered, before nodding her head.

'I didn't do anything,' said Dylan, throwing himself to the ground. 'I thought … maybe … it was a power I didn't know about … But it was you … even when we captured the Phantom Farter?'

'I just wanted to help,' she said meekly.

'Oh, this is BRILLIANT! Who cares about a stupid toothbrush plane when I've got you guys to entertain me! You guys KNOW each other, but she didn't tell you she was running around after you, cleaning up all your messes? Oh man, this is brilliant!' Mind

Bender said, rolling on the floor laughing.

Whilst Mind Bender was enjoying the moment, Cara continued. 'I'm sorry, truly I am, I never meant to make you feel bad, I just wanted to encourage you.'

'Wait, when I was fighting the Ice Cream Thief I heard a voice saying I needed to believe in myself …'

'That was me,' Cara said.

'And you stood up for me when that stupid Charlie Logan picked on me in class. I can't fight any of my own battles.'

'No,' she said firmly. 'Don't you understand? I'm not fighting your battles for you. No one can do that. I just want you to believe in yourself. You are a REAL-

LIFE SUPERHERO with an AWESOME superpower. You can achieve anything you set your mind to, and that includes defeating Mind Bender.' Dylan looked up for the first time. 'Believe, Dylan. BELIEVE!'

'Oh man, so, so, so good!' said Mind Bender, just about recovering as he got back to his feet. 'I'm going to have so much fun getting you two to do what I want ... YOU DIDN'T EVEN KNOW!!!' This sent him back into an uncontrollable fit of giggles.

Dylan composed himself, stood up straight and said, 'Well, I mean, I had wondered if she was a superhero, of course.'

'Oh, come on,' said Mind Bender, bringing the laughter under control. 'It's pretty obvious. You had absolutely no idea! This is HILARIOUS! Go on, just admit it ...'

'No,' said Dylan firmly. Mind Bender laughed heartily again, but then it began to fade as something started to dawn on him. The smile disappeared from his face as he looked at Dylan curiously.

'Admit it,' said Mind Bender firmly, taking a step towards Dylan.

'NO!' said Dylan, even stronger than the first time. Mind Bender furrowed his brow and snorted loudly in frustration.

'No one says no to me. EVER,' said Mind Bender, an angry frown appearing on his face.

'Really? That's strange because NO!' This

made Mind Bender jump.

'See … he can't control you, Dylan!' said Cara, understanding the situation perfectly. 'Your self-belief is too strong for him. Keep believing in yourself and resist him!'

Cara was right, thought Dylan. He really was resisting direct commands from Mind Bender. This was incredible!

'He can't control you? LET'S GET HIM!!!' screamed Red-Eye, who climbed on top of the sofa and threw himself towards Mind Bender. He stretched out his leg to do a kung-fu kick and landed a good three metres away from his intended target, crashing to the floor in a heap.

'Sorry, looks like he can control your

iguanas though,' said Cara.

'Nope, pretty certain that was all him,' said Dylan.

'Slap yourself!' said Mind Bender, who was beginning to panic.

'No,' said Dylan, gaining confidence. He took a step towards Mind Bender.

'Uh ... stop right there.' Dylan moved another step closer. He couldn't believe it. He was actually getting the upper hand against a supervillain all by himself. His belief in his own abilities grew stronger and stronger.

'You have him rattled, kid!' shouted Paul, urging him on. Dylan took another step towards him. This time, Mind Bender took a step backwards.

'Yeah, listen to his voice, word by word he is losing his conviction,' added Pauline. Dylan smiled. That was it. THAT was the source of his power. *Conviction.* Only Dylan had even more. He truly believed he could win.

'You know, I doubt you can actually *bend* minds,' said Dylan, grinning menacingly.

'I ... uh ... what does that matter?'

'So you admit it?'

'I didn't say that!'

'You can't though, can you? Go on, admit it.'

'I can't bend minds,' said Mind Bender. He put his hand to his mouth immediately. It was clear he hadn't meant to say that. It was like Dylan had forced him to do so, using his own power against him.

'You don't actually think you're going to win this battle, against the CITD, the BEST superhero team at the Superhero Collective?' asked Dylan, who was really in his element now. He had Mind Bender right where he wanted him.

'No ... I mean yes ... of course!' Mind Bender was beginning to sweat.

'And even if you did, do you seriously think you are going to get an electric toothbrush made of gold, which can turn into an aeroplane that can travel anywhere in the world in less than forty-five seconds?'

'No ... I mean NO! Wait, I meant to say

absolutely. Not. What is happening to me?!?'

'This is incredible, Dylan, it's all you! You're using his power against him!' said Cara, clapping her hands.

'Now, release all those superheroes from under your spell.' Dylan took a final step towards Mind Bender. He was now stood face to face with him; he could feel his breath on his face.

'I RELEASE YOU!' he screamed, before throwing himself to the floor, tears streaming down his cheeks.

The Telepathy Twins drew in a deep breath and hugged each other; Terrifying Suzanne let out an almighty scream; Cara disappeared and then reappeared instantly, checking to see her power still worked, and VentriloChris checked he had regained control of his arms by slapping himself in the face (this time he was in control of his hand though, so all was good).

The rest of the superheroes all did something similar, a check of their powers here, a check of their powers there, all except two: Dylan's brother and sister. Arctic Thunder huffed so hard in frustration at being saved by his dweeb of a brother (again) that a little bit of lightning escaped his nose. He hadn't been checking to see if his powers worked though, this was purely coincidental. Millie Monday on the other hand, well, let's just say it was a

Wednesday …

Arctic Thunder didn't stick around to thank his brother, flying straight up, crashing through the roof of the studio and making a swift (and rather unnecessary) exit.

'I'M GOING TO TEAR YOU APART, YOU FOOL!'

screamed Terrifying Suzanne, running full speed at Mind Bender. Just before she reached him, Dylan stepped out in front of her.

'STOP!' Terrifying Suzanne stopped dead in her tracks. 'Our job is to catch them and hand them over to the police, not to hurt them.'

'OUCH!' Mind Bender held the back of his

head, which was already beginning to swell having just been hit hard by a wellington boot.

'That's for taking over my studio and getting me to make you cups of tea,' said

Lauren Kelly before walking off in a huff.

'You got THE Lauren Kelly to make you tea? You deserved that, she's a national treasure!' said Paul.

'Please stop, don't hurt me!' pleaded Mind Bender.

'I feel like I need to hurt him now, to check he isn't still in control of me,' said VentriloChris.

'No, we don't need to. He won't control anyone else ever again. His power comes from conviction, and we've stripped that away from him. He is no longer a threat!' said Dylan confidently.

A little while later, the police arrived to take Mind Bender away. He asked them if they would mind not handcuffing him as he had 'sensitive wrists' but they simply laughed and tightened them. No one could doubt it now, his power was truly gone.

The rest of the superheroes approached Dylan and thanked him one by one. A queue had formed which stretched across the studio so each hero could pay their respects. Even his sister waited patiently in line.

'Thank you, Dy—' she began before remembering she wasn't meant to call him by his secret identity. 'Iguana Boy.' She smiled and walked away. It was a simple thank you, but it was the one that meant the most to him.

The last hero to approach was the

Outtatime Kid. 'Excellent work, brother,' he said, giving Dylan a big hug.

'I wish you were actually my brother, he couldn't even bring himself to say thank you,' said Dylan.

'Don't worry about him,' said the Outtatime Kid, putting a protective arm around his shoulder. 'Think back to how you felt when he was running around saving the world and you had no powers.'

'Mad with jealousy,' said Dylan, remembering it well. The Outtatime Kid raised his eyebrows and looked up to the Arctic Thunder-sized hole in the roof. He shrugged his shoulders as if to confirm his point.

'Thank you, I understand perfectly now,' said Dylan.

'You didn't the first fifteen times I tried, but you're welcome.' The Outtatime Kid shook Dylan's hand and then left the building, leaving Dylan with the iguanas, the CITD and ...

Cara. He had almost forgotten entirely about her. The invisible girl, hiding in plain sight all this time. The members of the CITD suddenly felt a little awkward and made their excuses to leave. Even VentriloChris picked up on the weird vibe, although saying, 'You know, there's a weird vibe here, I'm gonna shoot,' wasn't exactly a subtle way of leaving. The iguanas crawled into Dylan's bag and left the pair of them alone.

Dylan looked into Cara's eyes, and she looked back. They kept on staring, neither saying a word, not knowing where to begin.

'I ... uh ...' Dylan stalled his first attempt.

'It's not ...' Cara did the same.

'Thank you,' said Dylan, seemingly as surprised by the words that came from his mouth as Cara was.

'There's no need to thank me. I'm so sorry, I went about this completely the wrong way.'

'No,' said Dylan firmly, conviction still strong in his voice. 'You helped me learn a valuable lesson, you helped me to believe in myself, and a dangerous supervillain is behind bars because of it. I wouldn't change a single thing that happened.'

'Really?' she said brightly.

'Well, maybe I would change it so I wasn't hit in the head with a wellington boot,' he said thoughtfully, rubbing his forehead. The iguanas, who of course had been listening to the whole conversation (school bag material isn't exactly thick), emerged from his rucksack.

'Twice,' said Paul.

'Sorry about that,' added Pauline.

'Cara, meet my iguanas, Smelly Paul, Red-Eye, Pauline and Paul.'

'Paul. Great name for an iguana!'

Dylan smiled. 'I think you guys are going to get along famously.'

EPILOGUE

The sun was shining, and Dylan was sitting on the field at school breathing in the scent of freshly cut grass. He felt entirely at peace and it was a wonderful feeling. Sat next to him was his new best friend, although Dylan wasn't exactly aware of this ...

'Hey, Dylan!' said Cara, appearing beside

him. Dylan jumped to his feet, clutching his chest.

'How many times, Cara, please don't do that!' he said, calming down a little before sitting back down. He looked around. 'Besides, you've got to be careful, someone might see you.'

'It's unlikely, I am invisible after all,' she said, disappearing again. She reappeared on the other side of him. Dylan jumped, but not quite so much the second time.

'You know what I mean.'

'I do. Don't worry, I always look around before jumping out on you. I can't stop though, it's WAY too much fun ...'

Dylan smiled. It was really nice having a

friend at school, especially someone who knew his secret, someone he could confide in. In the weeks that followed, they had become best friends, always hanging out together both in and out of school. Dylan had even convinced her to join the Superhero Collective. She just needed a costume.

'I took on board what you said about the costume and I had this made,' said Cara, pulling out an all-in-one black suit. She held it up so Dylan could see. On the front was a large eye.

'Oh ...' said Dylan, looking a little embarrassed.

'You don't like it?'

'No ... I mean yes, I do, it's just I meant you

should have a large letter "I" for *Invisible* on the front, not an actual eye …'

'Oh … oops, well, I think it looks cool anyway,' she said with a sigh.

'Me too! Honestly, much better than what I said. Don't take advice from me anyway, my cape is an old picnic blanket …' They both laughed. 'You know, it's been great getting to know you these past few weeks, Cara, but there is something I've been meaning to ask you …'

'I was wondering when you were going to get the courage to ask,' she said, shuffling closer to him. Dylan's cheeks flushed red. 'You want to know how I knew you were Iguana Boy.'

'Yes, exactly! I just can't work it out.'

'It was pretty obvious, you talked about your iguanas ALL the time in class. You had four of them too, just like Iguana Boy.' Dylan looked a little embarrassed. 'Oh and one day, I saw one of them in your bag. They had obviously snuck in and you were NOT happy about it and you told them so. Looked like you guys were having a bit of an argument to be honest.'

'Fair enough,' said Dylan. As he said this, the iguanas all emerged from Dylan's bag.

'Yeah, you were NOT happy AT ALL when I snuck into your bag that day,' said Paul.

Dylan sighed heavily and Cara burst out

laughing.

'Really, guys, again?!?'

'We thought you might be missing us!' said Red-Eye.

'Yeah, and besides, I wanted to see what Cara's new costume looks like!' said Pauline, heading straight over to Cara and sitting on her shoulder. 'It's awesome!'

'Pauline likes your costume,' said Dylan.

'Hey, I do too!' said Smelly Paul, joining Pauline on Cara's shoulder.

'So does Smelly Paul,' he added.

'Wow, he really does smell ...'

'Why thank you,' said Smelly Paul, wrongly assuming that was a compliment. As he said this, a football flew over his head and hit

Dylan in the stomach, winding him. Dylan looked up to see Charlie Logan heading over, laughing as he ran. Cara covered up her costume, and the iguanas snuck back into Dylan's bag.

'Well, look who it is,' said Charlie, motioning for Dylan to throw him the ball. Dylan stood up gingerly and tossed the ball towards him. Instead of catching it, Charlie let the ball drop, and as it hit the ground, he kicked it at Dylan, hitting him in the stomach again.

'Hey!' said Cara, jumping to her feet. Dylan was hunched over holding his stomach with one arm, motioning to Cara to stop with the other.

'That wasn't nice,' said Dylan, picking up the ball.

'Oh sorry, I went to catch it and I missed. Then my foot slipped ...' Charlie laughed, as did the other football players who had gathered around. 'Throw it back, I'll catch it this time. I promise ...'

Dylan looked at Cara and smiled. He drew in a deep breath and then turned to face his tormentor.

'No,' said Dylan, standing tall. Charlie looked shocked.

'No? YOU don't say NO to me. Give. Me. The ball. NOW!'

'NO!' Dylan repeated confidently. Charlie took a step forward. Dylan took an even bigger step towards him.

'One last chance ...'

'OK, OK ...' said Dylan, finally giving in. He looked over at Cara, who was clearly worried. The iguanas were peeking out of the side of the bag too. He shot them all a wink then turned away. 'Here you go ...' said Dylan, before booting the ball high and far away over Charlie's head.

Charlie stared at Dylan, not believing what he was seeing. He looked directly into his eyes, and Dylan held his gaze, before taking a single step forward. Charlie stepped back, without even thinking.

'Yeah ... well ...' muttered Charlie, breaking his eyes away from the staredown.

He looked at his watch. 'Better finish this game, lads, only five minutes left of lunch.' Charlie turned away and ran after the football, shortly followed by the rest of the footballers.

When they were gone, the iguanas emerged from the bag cheering and doing backflips and other celebratory stuff that iguanas do. Cara was positively beaming.

'Way to go, Dylan, you gave him what for!' said Paul, jumping up on Dylan's shoulder.

'I knew you had it in you,' added Pauline. Red-Eye and Smelly Paul didn't say anything; they were dancing and it had somehow turned into a bit of a dance-off.

'He will leave you alone now,' added Cara.

'Bullies like him don't like confrontation. As soon as someone stands up to them, they back down. I'm really proud of you,' she said with a smile.

'Thanks, guys, but really it was easy,' said Dylan, dusting off his shoulders.

'Easy?!' said Paul, a little bemused.

'Yep. All I had to do was believe in myself.'

The End.

PS Oh … and Red-Eye TOTALLY won the dance-off. That iguana has some sick moves …

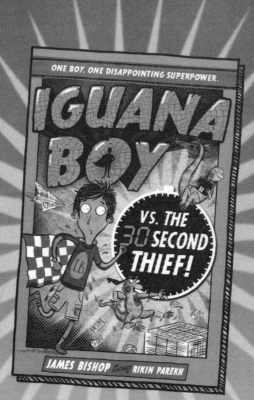

ONE BOY. ONE DISAPPOINTING SUPERPOWER.

IGUANA BOY

VS. THE 30 SECOND THIEF!

JAMES BISHOP AND ILLUSTRATED BY RIKIN PAREKH

JAMES BISHOP

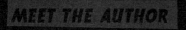

WHEN JAMES ISN'T BUSY
WRITING, HE CAN OFTEN BE FOUND
PLAYING FOOTBALL, DESPERATELY
TRYING NOT TO FALL OVER AND
MAKE A FOOL OF HIMSELF.

RIKIN PAREKH

WHEN RIKIN ISN'T BUSY
ILLUSTRATING, HE'S CHECKING
OUT LOCAL PIZZA RESTAURANTS
FOR THE BEST PIZZA IN TOWN.